Wonder Tales

Wonder Tales

Edited and introduced by

MARINA WARNER

with illustrations by
SOPHIE HERXHEIMER

Farrar, Straus and Giroux

NEW YORK

LIBRARY OF CONGRESS CATALOGING-IN-PUBLICATION DATA
Wonder tales / edited and introduced by Marina Warner ; with
illustrations by Sophie Herxheimer. — 1st American ed.
p.   cm.
Stories translated from the French.
Contents: The white cat / Marie-Catherine d'Aulnoy ; translated by
John Ashbery — The subtle princess / Marie-Jeanne L'Héritier de
Villandon ; translated by Gilbert Adair — Bearskin / Henriette-
Julie de Murat (attributed) ; translated by Terence Cave — The
counterfeit marquise / Charles Perrault & François-Timoléon de Choisy
(attributed) ; translated by Ranjit Bolt — Starlight / Henriette-Julie de
Murat (attributed) ; translated by Terence Cave — The great green worm /
Marie-Catherine d'Aulnoy ; translated by A. S. Byatt.
1. Fairy tales—France—Translations into English. 2. French fiction—
17th century—Translations into English. [1. Fairy tales.] I. Warner,
Marina. II. Herxheimer, Sophie, ill. III. Adair, Gilbert.

PQ1278. W66   1996
398.2'0944—dc20
96-14733
CIP
AC

For Carmen
With love, in wonder

CONTENTS

Introduction

Wonder has no opposite; it springs up already doubled in itself, compounded of dread and desire at once, attraction and recoil, producing a thrill, the shudder of pleasure and of fear. It names the marvel, the prodigy, the surprise as well as the responses they excite, of fascination and inquiry; it conveys the active motion towards experience and the passive stance of enrapturement. The French *conte de fées* is usually translated as fairy tale, but the word *Wundermärchen* was adopted by the Romantics in Germany and the Russian folklorists to characterise the folk tale or fairy tale. It's a useful term, it frees this kind of story from the miniaturised whimsy of fairyland to breathe the wilder air of the marvellous.

The six stories translated here were written in the heyday of the first literary enthusiasm for tales, by a group of writers who shared much else besides: they were urban, aristocratic, they knew one another's work, and exchanged ideas about it in various Parisian *hôtels particuliers* where they entertained; in some cases, they were close friends. It was these writers, almost all women, telling stories and publishing them in a city setting under the Sun King at a quintessential moment of the ancient régime, who consciously invented the modern fairy tale. Word games of all kind were a pastime, and the art of conversation developed as an ideal of salon society. Telling stories, elegantly, resourcefully, aptly, was required of a guest; in Mme de Murat's novel, *Les Lutins du château de Kernosy*, one of the heroine's unwanted suitors shows his dull wits when he fails to appreciate the importance of fantasy in narrative and goes to bed before the talespinning begins.

Charles Perrault, the famous author of *Contes du temps passé* (1697), in which the familiar versions of 'Cinderella', 'The Sleeping Beauty' and so forth first appeared, is represented here by a gallant tale on which he is now thought to have collaborated with a most remarkable spoiled priest and libertine, the Abbé de Choisy. Perrault championed the cause of the *conte de fées* against the scorn of his confrères in the Académie; he was a cousin of Marie-Jeanne L'Héritier and he responded to her ardent partisanship of the literary wonder tale. Furthermore, as the theme of 'The Counterfeit Marquise' is cross-dressing and Choisy was a celebrated transvestite, as Perrault also travestied himself in the guise of *ma Mère l'oye* (Mother Goose) to publish his tales, it didn't seem inappropriate to allow their story into a book otherwise composed by women, some of them countesses and baronesses, if not marquises.

More than the deeds of the fairies, wonders characterise fairy tales; indeed, fairies don't even put in an appearance sometimes (there are none in 'Red Riding Hood', for instance). But marvels of all kinds tumble (and fly) thick and fast through these stories, and various fairies, good and bad, appear to conjure them; they can offer help or hindrance, white magic or black magic; they form part of the intrinsic quest structure of the tales, as the protagonists are put to the test. The heroine must climb a mountain wearing iron shoes and fill a cribbled pail, she must go down to hell and fetch the magic water of discretion. The wonders also serve to punish the wicked – the ogre is deceived and beats thin air, thinking he is dispatching his enemy; sometimes they are both boon and bane, like the magic fruits in the fairies' garden in 'The White Cat', which come when you whistle.

Magic expresses itself above all in shape-shifting, and indeed, metamorphosis could be said to be one of the distinguishing marks of this protean genre; Bearskin, Starlight, The White Cat, Hidessa in 'The Great Green Worm', and the lovers in 'The Counterfeit Marquise' are all bound at one point or another in a different shape which conceals their true identity and their passion. The quest for love entails a quest for recognition of self, past the barriers of conventional expectation; love means that external social rules can be broken – the prince is disturbed by the desire that stirs in him for Bearskin in her mute bear form, and Izmir feels the attraction of Starlight when she's been turned into a Moor, contrary to her fear that he will not love her now that she has turned black. 'The Great Green Worm' is a tale of double metamorphosis in which both Hidessa, the ugly little one (Laidronette in the French) and the loathly worm find love before they are changed back into a fairy tale couple. All these transformations comment on the oppressive narrowness of the prevailing canon of beauty, the restrictive grasp of erotic possibilities. Although the tales are embedded in the values of their time, and bear the marks of its prejudices and its snobbery, they do also constantly press against the barriers to make them give way.

Hidessa is clever, and spirited and brave and persevering, and though Marie-Catherine d'Aulnoy was directly inspired by Apuleius's second-century tale of Cupid and Psyche, her heroine is never as lachrymose or spineless as poor Psyche; similarly, in

Marie-Jeanne L'Héritier's story, Finessa is full of schemes to fight adversity in whatever shape. The multiple masks and metamorphoses, ruses and disguises underline the importance of trueness of heart and toughness of mind, the inner world as opposed to the outer. But popular transmission of fairy tales, especially in the post-war period, has catastrophically emphasised beauty as the feminine virtue most needed to succeed. This runs directly counter to the vision of the female quester expressed here, above all by D'Aulnoy in 'The Great Green Worm'.

After wonder, consolation; after inquiry, resolution; after shape-shifting or metamorphosis, the happy ending. Happy endings characterise the wonder tale, and a happy ending, in this collection, means a certain strain of exalted, heartfelt, hardwon love. The formulaic closure of the traditional fairy tale has excited much criticism; especially from teachers who rightly deplore that such stories lead girl children to want wedding bells and nothing much else from life perhaps except a castle or two – the dream of becoming a Princess Di. This type of reading results when the tales are prised loose from their historical context, and viewed as unchanging repositories of eternal wisdom with application across time, place, culture, and history. Wonder tales do of course speak of things that matter and will go on mattering with universal significance; otherwise it wouldn't be possible to respond to the delicious fancifulness of 'The White Cat' with any pleasure today. But they were also produced for adults, to deal with actual, urgent dilemmas at a certain time and in a particular context, which shape and colour the obstacles and the goals of the heroes and the heroines. The modern residue, purveyed in a dozen Cinderella plots from Disney's film (1950) to *Pretty Woman* (1990), composed of sugarcandy ornament, ambitious snobbery, and demeaning romantic bilge misses the polished shafts the tales point at hypocrisy and greed and other social ills in their own times.

Though Henriette-Julie de Murat, Marie-Catherine d'Aulnoy, and Marie-Jeanne L'Héritier liked to stress that they told the stories to amuse, their material reveals the deep cunning of fiction and fantasy at work to give relief from pain. As Walter Benjamin has written, 'the original displeasure of anxiety' in wonder tales, 'turns into the great pleasure of anxiety successfully faced and mastered.' The *précieuses*, the feminist writers of the generation before D'Aulnoy and L'Héritier, had fought for tenderness in friendship between men and women, for reform of the language, and for equal rights to intelligent talk. They had also focused on matters of more immediate material urgency: asking for control of their own money, for their right to choose not to marry; or, if they were married off, they wanted to be given the same social permission, as men, to take a lover. Above all, however, they wanted to decide for themselves on the husband of their choice, not accept an arrangement with a stranger. They also sued for the opportunity to learn, and to travel. These demands are buried in the tales; they were driven into the coded language of enchantment by the most penetrative state censorship on the one hand, and fervent religious revivalism on the other. They themselves had to undergo metamorphosis and hide in the landscape of wonder in the later years of the Sun King's reign – Marie-Jeanne L'Héritier was a *salonnière*, who inherited the salon held by the novelist and high priestess of the *précieuses* movement, Madeleine de Scudéry. The Baronne d'Aulnoy received in her successful salon on the rue St Benoît; Perrault and the Abbé de Choisy frequented these social gatherings; so did Mme de Murat, until she was exiled from Paris by order of the king, because she had written a satire which clearly targeted his liaison with the pious Mme de Maintenon. Murat was sent to Loches, in the

Loire valley, in 1694, and was held there under a form of house arrest; nevertheless, she began her own 'Académie du domicile' to keep herself amused, and was remembered by one friend as telling stories at night till the embers in the fire died out.

Murat's disgrace offers a precious insight into the immediate context of the wonder tales collected here. The *salons* and the *salonnières* were watched by the court at Versailles (Anne of Austria was known to have hired spies to infiltrate them because they were seedbeds of protest and dissent); the Fronde, the nobles' uprising which convulsed the early part of Louis XIV's reign, had been organised from the salons of great ladies, like the Marquise de Rambouillet – some of them famously took part in the fighting.

The positions developed in salon conversation were not intrinsically or exclusively political – they were socially subversive. The practice of storytelling grew up in the salons as part of an open campaign about equality and intelligence in conversation; the *précieuses*, with Madeleine de Scudéry at their head, assaulted the conventions which made *galanteries* the only topic of mixed company. It is hard for readers today, accustomed to the frivolous image of the ancien régime, to pass through the screen of custom and rethink the character of some of its personalities. The rise of rationalist philosophers helped to distort their activities, especially their use of fantasy, and their love of extravagant storytelling. Rousseau would proscribe fairy tales from children's education in *Émile*; such nonsense could overheat their already excited minds, he argued. He also scorned the salons for their effeminacy: 'Every woman in Paris,' he wrote, 'gathers in her apartment a harem of men more womanish than she.' He recommended that men retire to their own clubs, according to the English model. The Marquise de Lambert, one of the great literary ladies of the salons, was already lamenting at the start of the eighteenth century, 'There were, in an earlier time houses where [women] were allowed to talk and think, where the muses joined the society of the graces. The Hôtel de Rambouillet, greatly honoured in the past century, has become the ridicule of ours.'

Henriette-Julie de Murat was not alone in using tales to catch the conscience of the king; nor in being punished for it. The seventeenth-century wonder tale, with its varied register, now *galant*, now caustic, now knowing, now faux-naïf, points forward to the biting Voltairean conte. Voltaire was friends with his storyteller contemporaries, like Mlle de Lubert, who were carrying on the ironic tradition adumbrated by D'Aulnoy and Murat, and straining medieval fable and romance through a mesh of satire. In Murat's novel, *Les Lutins du château de Kernosy*, the two stories 'Starlight' and 'Bearskin' are told aloud to the company gathered after dinner: including the heroines' aunt and guardian, who has plans to sell her wards to the highest bidder, however appalling he might be, in order to pay off her gambling debts. (Though these tales have been reattributed to Lubert since, they function seamlessly within Murat's scheme.)

The pioneering D'Aulnoy also focuses on impediments to love. She recast the classical love story of Cupid and Psyche in a myriad tales, obsessively making the case for choice against the intrigues of interested parties. In her *contes*, like 'The Great Green Worm' and 'The White Cat', true love has to struggle against numerous determined enemies. Though the message is largely lost on today's audience, thoroughly accustomed to choosing not just one partner but several, the French wonder tale was fighting for social emancipation and change on grounds of urgent personal experience.

Marie-Catherine d'Aulnoy was fifteen or sixteen in 1666, when she was taken from a convent where she had been placed for her education by François de la Motte, Baron d'Aulnoy, some thirty years older than her, who had bought his title and his lands after rising from the position of valet in the service under of the Duc de Vendôme, a nobleman well-known for his taste in young men. In her *Memoirs*, which are as colourful as her wonder tales might lead one to expect, she relates how she was abducted without warning with the connivance of her father, who profited in the transaction. Three years later – this part does not appear in the *Memoirs* – Marie-Catherine d'Aulnoy became entangled in a remarkable scandal. In 1669, two noblemen deposed against M. le Baron d'Aulnoy that, in a fit of rage against a tax demand which he was refusing to pay, he had abused the king and his ministers in the Palais de Luxembourg. Their testimony landed the baron in the Bastille on a charge of lèse-majesté, which then carried a capital penalty. He escaped death after the witnesses against him had been tortured and confessed to calumny. Their testimonial implicated Marie-Catherine d'Aulnoy and her mother, the Marquise de Gadagne, as fellow conspirators: the men were believed to be their lovers, and the whole incident an elaborate and careful scheme to rid themselves of M. d'Aulnoy.

The two women left the country; again, the scraps of evidence read like an adventure – out of Alexandre Dumas, however, rather than the seventeenth century. One story describes how Mme d'Aulnoy was in bed when the sergeant arrived to arrest her, how she jumped out of the window, and hid under a bier in a nearby church, before rejoining her mother and fleeing abroad. Later, Mme de Gadagne was given a handsome pension by the king of Spain for services rendered in Rome; her daughter returned to Paris around 1685, no questions asked, and opened her salon, where she enjoyed dressing up with her guests as characters in the stories they exchanged, between refreshments of fruit cordials, café au lait, and hot chocolate.

Mother and daughter had been reprieved, it was said, on condition they worked as spies for the French, and that they lived (and pursued their trade) in Spain, Italy and England. The Baron d'Aulnoy did not receive much sympathy; on his death in 1700, Saint-Évremond wrote to his widow (there was no possibility of divorce), 'The condition of a widowhood . . . brings joy to those who lose wicked husbands.' He added that he was sorry that she had been left nothing: 'This injustice alone makes me loathe his memory.' Deprived of marital support (in the circumstances perhaps not surprising), need drove on Mme d'Aulnoy's industry. She had a light-fingered way with sources, and her first great successes – spirited and apparently first-hand accounts of manners and morals at the Spanish and English courts – have been shown to be either fanciful – or borrowed. Such stratagems are quite proper, however, in the fantastic sphere of the wonder tale; D'Aulnoy recasts the ancient folk tales and romances she discovered with her own rampant imagination, laced with mordancy, and bubbling with fantastical invention.

Marie-Catherine d'Aulnoy's is an exceptional story in its detail, but not in its general drift; the Comtesse de Murat was denounced for unruly behaviour, including lesbianism, by her husband and his family, and after long petitioning, only succeeded in returning to Paris from exile a year before she died. The account of the ogre Rhinoceros in 'Starlight' and of parents who oppose their son's wishes in 'Bearskin' and renege on their promises, springs from the same social arrangements as D'Aulnoy's tales, which for all their high-spirited fun, can sound a dark note at times: 'Such a marriage becomes slavery if it is not formed by love.'

These successors of the *précieuses* were combating aristocratic complacency and determinism: tenderness and interior worth rather than title and goods were what they urged in a prospective husband. It's a matter of historical irony typical of women's lives that these women should be known by their married names and titles – but the situation is difficult to reverse in library catalogues and other reference works. L'Héritier, by contrast, like one or two other contemporaries whose work is still little known (Mlle de Lubert and Mlle Bernard) resisted marriage throughout her life, following the example of her friend and mentor Mlle de Scudéry.

Men and matrimony were not the only issue to which the women developed responses in common. The ironical picture of Quietlife Island in 'Starlight' comments for instance on Louis XIV's ruinous wars and the cult of military might. But their storytelling presented a united front in other ways, too.

Wonder tales and fairy stories do not have onlie begetters, but are reworked from tradition and other sources, and crystallised in one form at one time by one teller for one audience, then by another with different listeners or readers in mind. The stories here share a declared origin in tradition: D'Aulnoy claims in one place to have gathered her material from 'an old Arab slave woman', L'Héritier invokes more intimate memories of her own nurse and governess telling her stories by the fire, and she urged her friend the Comtesse de Murat to follow her example and set down on paper the ancient tales which had come down in French from the voices of the people; Murat caused a commotion in Paris when she went out wearing the Breton peasant costume she favoured. The *conte* was characteristically transmitted orally, and when Marie-Jeanne L'Héritier and Murat made their claim to popular roots, they were defying the tradition of high-flown classicism, pompous odes and allegorising mythologies. Fables, old wives' tales, proverbs, the handed-down, well-used, anonymous culture did not require an education to be understood or an aristocratic audience to be heard; the writers shared it among themselves, and echoes sound between the stories, as the imagery recurs, of white cats, disembodied hands, rudderless boats, while the motifs return with modular differences: cannibal ogres, jealous old fairies, bad mothers, rivalrous brothers. 'The White Cat' for instance recognisably combines the plots of 'Rapunzel' and 'The Three Feathers', two of the best-known Grimm Brothers' tales, published much later, in 1812.

The popular, unwritten provenance was often – almost always – fictive. D'Aulnoy drew on Greek romances, medieval legends of Mélusine, on Tristan and on Merlin, on *fabliaux* and the *Lais* of Marie de France, on her contemporary La Fontaine, as well as finding plots and much narrative incident in the down-to-earth and vigorous fantasies of story collections like Boccaccio's *Decameron* and *Le Piacevoli Notti* by Giovan Francesco Straparola ('The Babbler'). L'Héritier, too, for all her protestations about her beloved childhood nurse, also drew on printed literature, especially Giambattista Basile's *Lo Cunto de li Cunti*, published in 1634–6 in Naples. She chose to pass on Basile's tale 'Sapia Liccarda' because it features a heroine of spirit resisting her given fate. But she made changes. The wicked brother does not figure in the earlier Italian story, and all the heroine's tricks are only her ardent way of testing her lover. L'Héritier's rather gruesome additions – in the Basile, the dummy is made of sweetmeats, in 'The Subtle Princess', of animal lights – confront the existence of unregenerate, male wickedness. Although the flavour of her style and her friends' and colleagues' remains unequivocally literary, even flowery, it is also garrulous; repetition and hyperbole, cascades of detail in description, and circles within circles of plot devices are all part of the bazaar storyteller's stock-in-trade. These authors further laid claim to an oral context of origin, by framing several of these tales within a novel, in which one of the characters is given a turn to tell a story aloud. To keep this particular stylistic flavour, dialogue has been set out in this collection as if the stories were being told by one voice.

The hard and fast distinction between literature and orature breaks down in the tradition, because the written versions nourish the spoken and vice versa. 'Starlight' rings changes on the medieval *chante-fable* of 'Aucassin and Nicolette', including the topsy-turvy land, Quietlife Island, where the women do the fighting (with crab apples) while the menfolk lie around in bed. Variations on the theme of the trickster princess who lives on her wits, dupes her adversaries with dummies and masks in order to win her true love, appear all over the world and are still being told aloud today. A story recently collected in Palestine relates with similar glee the clever ruses of a certain Sahin, to win herself and her sisters well-trained husbands.

The point of recalling the oral connection was twofold: as women writers and fairy tales were sneered at by members of the Académie française like Boileau, they made common cause by identifying themselves with the vulgar people against the establishment authorities, who debarred them. In the prolonged and bitter Querelle des Anciens et des Modernes (The Quarrel between the Ancients and the Moderns) women and wonders were fiercely, definitely Modern; men and gods Ancient. Madame de Lafayette, even though her chaste restraint tends to the *ancien* style, was influenced by the circle of *modernes* in which she had earlier moved, to catch an atmosphere of wonder here and there.

But also, by pleading native, Gallic tradition, the storytellers could include anything and everything they pleased, breaking all the rules of classicism, of the unities, of linguistic purity, of decorum – what was called *bienséance* or seemliness. Hence the pleasure in the grotesque, the unlikely and the incongruous, the mixture of tragedy and comedy, the frank eroticism, the casual cruelty and the topsy-turvy bizarreries in these tales of wonder: nothing could be further from the austere tenor and proportion of a tragedy by Racine.

The challenge issued by the form of the *conte* or wonder tale itself has been overlooked in the subsequent domestication of the genre; when the child audience was singled out by the newly flourishing market in juvenile literature, fairy tales began to be adapted to suit a nursery setting, with patent moralities adjusted to train children in what is expected of them. This trend started in the chapbooks of the eighteenth century but was established in the first quarter of the nineteenth. D'Aulnoy remained the most successful of the writers in the new, fashionable genre, but her work was continually abridged and bowdlerised – with the paradoxical effect of making it seem all frills and furbelows and bo-peep bonnets. 'Mother Bunch', the sobriquet she was given in eighteenth-century England, became a portmanteau name, like Mother Goose, for a fairy storyteller; when she was still alive, Mme d'Aulnoy tried unavailingly to unscramble the false attributions and the pirated editions. Though the tradition of storytelling should entail a continual return, reclaim, revision, and maybe repudiation, it is a pity when the palimpsest becomes so dense that the text beneath is obscured.

Perrault is today much more famous than Madame d'Aulnoy or the other writers published in this collection, partly because he too was adapted, modified, and carefully selected over centuries of popular publication. The cannibal ogress in 'The Sleeping Beauty' has been cut from many later editions, for instance, and the tale included here has never been included in a collection of Perrault's *Contes* even though the best scholarship has attributed it to him. Though Perrault's ambiguous approach to the nursery tale was always clear to the reader, he became a favourite uncle because his jocular tone pokes fun at the material itself (when the ogre's wife in Hop O' My Thumb finds her daughters' throats cut, she has a fainting fit – 'most women faint in similar circumstances' remarks Perrault). This sprightliness covers up the darkness lurking in his stories (the cruelty to Cinderella, the incest in 'Donkeyskin'), in a way that Madame d'Aulnoy's fantasies never do. Her ironies reinforce the viciousness or indifference of her wicked characters rather than work to blur their impact.

The writers collected in *Wonder Tales* were anthologised in *Le Cabinet des Fées*, first published in three volumes in Amsterdam in 1731, then rearranged and increased to forty-one volumes and appearing from 1785 in Paris and Amsterdam and then in Geneva, after the Revolution interrupted their appearance. The attributions were muddled, and have continued to present some problems: 'The Subtle Princess' for instance was given to Murat in 1731, to Perrault in 1785, though the editor there admitted he was not sure Perrault had written it; the first edition of Murat's novel, *Les Lutins du château de Kernosy* (1710), does not include the two tales printed here. D'Aulnoy's tales filled one volume in the 1731 edition of *Le Cabinet*, and nearly four in 1785. Jack Zipes, the American folklore scholar, has recently retrieved many of these neglected authors for the contemporary, English-speaking audience with his collections; this book owes a great debt to his pioneering work. 'Bearskin' and 'Starlight' have never been reprinted in French, let alone translated, as they were not collected with Murat's stories in *Le Cabinet des Fées*, where she fills the first two volumes of the 1731 edition.

Terence Cave, who has made a subtle and impeccable translation of 'The Princesse de Clèves', by Mme de Lafayette, seemed the appropriate choice for these urbane and ironic romances. Gilbert Adair, who enjoys intertextual games, responded to Marie-Jeanne L'Héritier; three hundred years ago she ended one story with the self-reflexive comment: 'If, like many travellers in the land of Fiction, my fate is to get lost in this land, more difficult to cross than people think, it's as well that I get lost on the path I've chosen, than on another.' Ranjit Bolt, who has turned such adroit versions of plays by Perrault's contemporaries like Molière, has translated the Perrault–Choisy, with its dramatic disguises, mistaken identities and climactic final curtain. A. S. Byatt, who in *Possession* explored the serpentine lore of the fairy Mélusine, and even named her heroine the poet Christabel LaMotte, has written fairy tales herself, and in her recent novella, 'Morpho Eugenia' in *Angels and Insects*, played her own enigma variations on the butterfly imagery of Cupid and Psyche; D'Aulnoy might have scried Byatt in a magic glass when she was writing 'Le Serpentin vert'. At a launch of his book of poems, *Flow Chart*, John Ashbery revealed that he was translating 'The White Cat' for the sheer delight of it – a piece of strong and magic luck which set this book on its way, as the first volume, it is hoped, of a new library of the wonder tale.

MARINA WARNER
Kentish Town, 1993

the queen, anxious to slake
her craving, flung herself on them.

✷ *The White Cat*

Translated by John Ashbery

MARIE-CATHERINE D'AULNOY

There was once a king who had three sons, stout and courageous lads; he feared lest the desire to reign might overtake them before his death; there were even rumours that they were seeking to acquire vassals, so as to deprive him of his kingdom. The king felt his age, yet he was still sound of mind and body, and by no means inclined to surrender a position he filled with much dignity; therefore he concluded that the best way to live in peace was to tease them with promises which he would always be able to avoid fulfilling.

He summoned them to his chamber, and after having spoken to them in a most kindly manner, he added: You will no doubt agree with me, dear children, that my advanced age no longer allows me to pursue affairs of state with the zeal of times gone by; I am afraid that my subjects may suffer because of this, and wish to place my crown on the head of one or another of you; but it is only right that, in view of such a prize, you seek various ways of pleasing me, even as I prepare my plans for retiring to go and live in the country. It seems to me that a little dog, one that is faithful, clever and pretty, would keep me company very well;

hence without choosing my eldest son, neither my youngest, I declare to you that whichever of you three brings me the most beautiful little dog will at once become my heir. The princes were surprised by their father's inclination to have a little dog, but the two younger ones might turn it to their advantage, and accepted with pleasure the commission to go to look for one; the eldest was too timid or too respectful to argue his rights. They took leave of the king; he gave them money and jewels, stipulating that they return without fail in a year, on the same day and at the same hour, to bring him their little dogs.

Before setting out they betook themselves to a castle at only a league's distance from the city. They brought their closest confidants with them, and, amid much feasting, each brother swore eternal loyalty to the others, that they would proceed to act without jealousy or bitterness, and that the most fortunate would always share his fortune with the others; finally they went away, promising that on their return they would reassemble in the same castle before going together to meet their father; they wanted no one to accompany them, and changed their names so as not to be recognised.

Each journeyed by a different route: the two eldest had many adventures; but I am concerned only with those of the youngest. He was gracious, with a merry and witty temperament and a handsome mien; his body was nobly proportioned, his features regular, he had beautiful teeth, and much skill in all the activities that befit a prince. He sang agreeably; he plucked the lute and the theorbo with a delicate touch that people found charming. He knew how to paint; in a word, he was highly accomplished; and as for his valour, it verged on fearlessness.

Hardly a day passed without his buying dogs, big ones, little ones, greyhounds, mastiffs, bloodhounds, hunting dogs, spaniels, barbets, lapdogs; no sooner had he found a handsome one than he found one handsomer still, and parted with the first so as to keep the other; for it would have been impossible for him to travel with thirty or forty thousand dogs, and he wanted neither gentlemen-in-waiting, nor menservants, nor pages in his retinue. He kept pushing forward, with no idea of where he was going; suddenly he was overtaken by darkness, thunder and rain, in a forest whose paths he could no longer make out.

He took the first road he came upon, and after walking for a long time he spied a dim light, which convinced him that there must be a house near by where he might take shelter until the morrow. Guided by the light, he arrived at the gate of a castle, the most magnificent one that could ever be imagined. The gate was made of gold, studded with carbuncles, whose pure and vivid glow illuminated the whole vicinity. It was the one the prince had glimpsed from far away; the castle walls were of translucent porcelain in which various colours were mingled, and on which was depicted the history of all the fairies, from the creation of the world down to the present: the famous adventures of Peau d'Ane, of Finessa, of the Orange Tree, of Graciosa, of the Sleeping Beauty, of the Great Green Worm, and of a hundred others, were not omitted. He was delighted to recognise the Goblin Prince, for the latter was his first cousin once removed. The rain and the stormy weather prevented him from tarrying further while getting drenched to the bone, besides which he could see nothing at all in places where the light of the carbuncles didn't penetrate.

He returned to the golden gate; he saw a deer's hoof fastened to a chain made entirely of diamonds; he wondered at the negligence of those who lived in the castle; for, he said to himself, what is there to prevent thieves from coming to cut away the chain and rip out the carbuncles? They would be rich forever.

He pulled on the deer's hoof, and at once heard the tinkling of a bell, which must have been gold or silver judging from the tone; after a moment the door opened, but he saw naught but a dozen hands that floated in the air, each holding a torch. He was so astonished that he paused at the threshold, and then felt other hands pushing him from behind with some violence. He went forward in trepidation, and, as a precaution, placed his hand on the hilt of his sword; but on entering a vestibule all encrusted with porphyry and lapis, he heard two ravishing voices singing these words:

> Fear not these hands in the air,
> And in this dwelling place
> Fear naught but a lovely face
> If your heart would flee love's snare.

He could hardly believe that such a gracious invitation would bring him harm; and feeling himself pushed towards an enormous gate of coral, which opened as soon as he approached, he entered a salon panelled with mother-of-pearl, and then several chambers variously decorated, and so rich with paintings and precious stones, that he experienced a kind of enchantment. Thousands of lights attached to the walls, from the vaulted ceiling down to the floor, lit up parts of the other apartments, which were themselves filled with chandeliers, girandoles, and tiers of candles; in sum, the magnificence was such that he could scarcely believe his eyes, even as he looked at it.

After he had passed through sixty chambers, the hands ceased to guide him; he saw a large easy chair, which moved all by itself close to the hearth. At the same moment the fire lit itself, and the hands, which seemed to him very beautiful, white, small, plump, and well proportioned, undressed him, for he was drenched as I have already said, and feared he might catch cold. He was given, without his seeing anybody, a shirt splendid enough to wear on one's wedding day, and a dressing gown made of cloth-of-gold, embroidered with tiny emeralds which formed numbers. The disembodied hands brought him a table on which his toilet articles were laid out. Nothing could have been more elegant; they combed his hair with a deft and light touch which pleased him mightily. Then they clothed him anew, but not with his own clothes; much richer ones had been provided. He silently admired everything that was happening around him, and sometimes he succumbed to shudders of fear that he was not quite able to suppress.

After he had been powdered, curled, perfumed, decked out, tidied up, and rendered more handsome than Adonis, the hands led him into a salon that was superbly gilded and furnished. All round the room one saw the histories of the most famous Cats: Rodillardus* hanged by his paws at the council of rats; Puss-in-Boots of the Marquis de Carabas; the scrivener Cat; the Cat who turned into a woman, witches turned into cats, the witches' sabbath and all its ceremonies; in a word, nothing was more remarkable than these pictures.

The table had been laid; there were two places, each set with a golden casket which held the knives, forks and spoons; the buffet astonished him with its abundance of rock-crystal vases and a thousand rare gems. The prince was wondering for whom these two places were laid, when he saw cats taking their place in a small orchestra set up just for the occasion; one held up a score covered with the most extraordinary notes in the world; another a scroll of paper which he used to beat time; the others had small guitars. Suddenly each one began to miaow in a different key, and to scratch the guitar strings with their claws; it was the strangest music ever heard. The prince would have thought himself in hell, had he not found the palace too wonderful to admit of such an unlikely circumstance; but he stopped his ears and laughed uncontrollably as he watched the various posturings and grimaces of these newfangled musicians.

He was reflecting on the queer things that had already happened to him in this castle, when he saw a tiny figure scarcely a cubit in height entering the room. This puppet was draped in a long veil of black crêpe. Two cats attended her; they were dressed in mourning, wearing cloaks, with swords at their side; a large cortège of cats followed; some carried rat traps filled with rats, others brought mice in cages.

The prince was struck dumb with amazement; he knew not what to think. The black figurine approached, lifting its veil, and he perceived the most beautiful White Cat that ever was or ever will be. She appeared to be very young and very sad; she began to miaow so gently and sweetly that it went straight to his heart; she spoke to the prince: Welcome, O king's son; my miaowing majesty is pleased with the sight of you. Madam Cat, said the prince, you are most generous to receive me with so much hospitality, but you seem to be no ordinary beastie; your gift of speech and the superb castle you own are evident proofs of this. King's son, replied the White Cat, I pray you, pay me no more compliments; I am simple in my speech and my manners, but my heart is kind. Come, she continued, let dinner be served, and let the musicians cease, for the prince doesn't understand what they are saying. And are they saying something, Madam? he enquired. I am sure they are, she continued; we have poets here gifted with infinite powers of wit, and if you rest awhile among us, you will have cause to be convinced. I have only to listen to you to believe it, said the prince gallantly; but then, Madam, I consider you a rare Cat indeed.

Supper was brought in; the hands whose bodies were invisible served it. First, two bisques were placed on the table, one of pigeon, the other of well-fattened mice. The sight of one prevented the prince from tasting the other, for he supposed that the same cook had prepared them both: but the little Cat, who guessed what his thoughts were from the face he made, assured him that his meal was cooked separately, and that he could eat what was served him, in the certitude that there would be neither rats nor mice in it.

The prince didn't have to be asked twice, sure in his belief that the pretty little Cat had no intention of deceiving him. He noticed a tiny portrait painted on metal that she wore at her wrist, which surprised him. He begged her to show it to him, imagining that it must be a portrait of Master Minagrobis,* the

king of the Cats. What was his astonishment to find it that of a young man so handsome that it seemed scarcely possible that nature might have formed another like him, yet who resembled him so strongly that one couldn't have portrayed him better.

She sighed, and becoming more melancholy, kept a profound silence. The prince realised that there was something extraordinary in all this; however he dared not enquire what it was, for fear of displeasing the Cat, or distressing her. He chatted with her, telling her all the news he knew, and found her well versed in the different interests of princes, and of other things that were going on in the world.

After supper, the White Cat invited her guest into a salon where there was a stage, on which twelve cats and twelve monkeys were dancing a ballet. The former were in Moorish costume, the latter in Chinese. It is easy to imagine the sort of leaps and capers they executed, while from time to time clawing at one another; it was thus that the evening came to an end. White Cat bade goodnight to her guest; the hands that had guided him thus far took over once again and led him to an apartment that was the exact opposite of the one he had seen. It was not so much magnificent as elegant; the whole was papered with butterfly wings, whose diverse colours formed a thousand different flowers. There were also feathers of extremely rare birds, which perhaps had never been seen except in that place. The bed was draped with gauze, attached by thousands of knotted ribbons. There were enormous mirrors extending from the ceiling to the parquet, and their borders of chased gold depicted an immense crowd of little cupids.

The prince lay down without saying a word, for there was no way of making conversation with the hands that waited on him; he slept little, and was awakened by an indistinct noise. The hands immediately drew him from his bed and dressed him in a hunter's habit. He looked out into the courtyard of the castle and saw five hundred cats, some of whom had greyhounds on a leash, while others were sounding the horn; it was a great celebration. White Cat was going hunting; she wanted the prince to come with her. The officious hands presented him with a wooden horse which galloped and cantered marvellously; he was somewhat reluctant to mount it, saying that he was far from being a knight errant like Don Quixote; but his resistance was useless, and they placed him on the wooden horse. It had a cloth and a saddle made of gold-lace embroidery and diamonds. White Cat mounted a monkey, the handsomest and most superb ever seen; she had removed her long veil and wore a dragon's hood, which lent her an air so resolute that all the mice in the region were afraid. Never was a hunting party more agreeable; the cats ran faster than the rabbits and hares, so that when they caught one, White Cat had the spoils divided up before her, and a thousand amusing tricks of dexterity were performed; the birds for their part weren't too secure, for the kittens climbed the trees, and the chief monkey bore White Cat up as far as the eagles' nests, so that she might dispose of the little eagle highnesses according to her whim.

Once the hunt was over, she picked up a horn the length of a finger, but which gave out such a high, clear sound that it was easily audible ten leagues hence; no sooner had she sounded two or three fanfares than she was surrounded by all the cats in the land; some travelled by air, ensconced in chariots; others by water in barques; in a word, so many cats had never been seen before. Almost all were dressed in different costumes; she returned to the castle in pomp with this cortège, and invited the prince to come too. He was willing, even though all this cat business smacked a bit of sorcery and the witches' sabbath, and the talking cat astonished him more than anything else.

As soon as they were back at the castle, her great black veil was placed over her head; she supped with the prince, who was hungry; liqueurs were brought which he drank with pleasure, and instantly they blotted out the memory of the little dog which he was to bring back to the king. He no longer thought of anything but miaowing with White Cat, that is, of being her good and faithful companion; he spent the days in agreeable pastimes, sometimes he went fishing or hunting; or ballets and chariot races would be staged, and a thousand other diversions to his liking; often the beautiful Cat would even compose verses and ditties in a style so passionate that one might have thought her in love, that one couldn't speak as she did without being in love; but her secretary, an old cat, wrote so illegibly that, even though these works have been preserved, it is impossible to read them.

The prince had even forgotten his country. The hands of which I have spoken continued to serve him. Sometimes he was sorry not to be a cat, so as to spend his life in such delightful company. Alas! he said to White Cat, how sorrowful I shall be when I leave you; I love you so dearly. Either become a girl, or turn me into a cat. She found his request most amusing, and gave only obscure answers, of which he understood almost nothing.

A year passes quickly when one has no cares or worries, when one is happy and in good health. White Cat knew the date when he must return, and as he no longer thought about it, she reminded him. Do you know, she said, that you have but three days to find the little dog that the king your father wants, and that your brothers have found very handsome ones? The prince came to his senses, amazed at his own negligence: By what secret charm, he exclaimed, have I forgotten the thing in the world that matters most to me? My kingdom and my glory depend on it; where will I find a dog that will win me a kingdom, and a horse swift enough to travel such a long way? He began to worry, and was sore aggrieved.

White Cat told him, in gentler tones: King's son, cease

lamenting, I am on your side; you may stay another day here, and, although your country is five hundred leagues distant, the trusty wooden horse will bear you there in less than twelve hours. I thank you, lovely Cat, said the prince; but it isn't enough for me to return to my father's house; I must also bring him a little dog. Ha! replied White Cat, here is an acorn inside which you'll find one more beautiful than the dog star itself. Oh, said the prince, Madam Cat, your majesty is making fun of me. Put the acorn next to your ear, she continued, and you'll hear him yap. He obeyed: at once the tiny dog began to yip and yap; the prince was transported with joy, since a dog that can be contained in an acorn must be tiny indeed. He wished to open it, but White Cat told him the dog might catch cold during the trip: it would be better to wait until he was in the presence of his father the king. He thanked her a thousand times, and bade her a most tender adieu; I assure you, he said, that the days with you have seemed so short that I quite regret leaving you behind, and though you be the sovereign here, and all the cats who attend to you are much wittier and gallant than our courtiers, I cannot resist inviting you to come with me. The Cat replied to this suggestion with nothing more than a profound sigh.

They took leave of each other; the prince arrived first at the castle where the meeting with his brothers was to take place. They arrived soon after, and were astonished to find a wooden horse in the courtyard who pranced better than any of those in the riding academies.

The prince came out to greet them. They embraced each other several times and recounted their various travels; but our prince took care not to tell the true story of his adventures, and showed them an ugly cur that was used for turning a spit, saying he had found it so pretty that he had decided to bring it to the king.

Despite the affection that united them, the two brothers felt a secret joy at their brother's ill-advised choice; they were at table and trod on each other's feet, as though to tell each other they had nothing to fear from that quarter.

The next day they left together in the same coach. The two elder sons of the king had little dogs in baskets, so beautiful and so delicate that one would scarcely have dared to touch them. The youngest brought his poor turnspit, so filthy that no one could stand him. Once they were inside the palace, everyone gathered round to welcome them; they entered the king's apartment. He couldn't decide which of them to favour, for the little dogs that the two eldest proffered him were almost of equal beauty, and already they were arguing over which of them would inherit the crown, when the youngest settled their dispute by drawing from his pocket the acorn that White Cat had given him. He opened it at once, and everyone saw a tiny dog lying on a bed of cotton wool. He stepped through a finger ring without touching it. The prince set him on the floor, and at once he began to dance the saraband with castanets, as deftly as the most renowned Spanish dancer. His coat was of a thousand different colours; his fur and his tail trailed along the ground. The king was profoundly abashed, for it was impossible to find anything to criticise in this beautiful doggie.

And yet he had no wish to part with his crown. Its least rosette
was dearer to him than all the dogs in the universe. So he told his
sons that he was satisfied with their efforts, but that they had
succeeded so well in the first task he had set them that he wanted
to test their cleverness further before keeping his word; and so he
was giving them a year to search by land and sea for a piece of
cloth so fine that it would pass through the eye of a Venetian
lace-maker's needle. All three were sorely distressed at being
obliged to set out on a new quest. The two princes, whose dogs
were less handsome than their younger brother's, gave their
assent. Each went off in a different direction, with fewer friendly
effusions than the first time, as the turnspit had somewhat cooled
their affections.

Our prince set off on his wooden horse, and without caring to
seek other help than that he could expect from the White Cat's
friendship, returned to the castle where she had so cordially
received him. He found all the doors open; the windows, the
roofs, the towers and the walls were lit by a hundred thousand
lamps, which produced a marvellous effect. The hands that had
served him so well before came to meet him, took the bridle of
the excellent wooden horse and led him to the stable, while the
prince entered the chamber of the White Cat.

She was lying in a little basket, on a mattress of spotless white
satin. Her nightcap was somewhat askew, and she seemed
dejected; but when she noticed the prince she did a thousand
leaps and as many capers, to show him how happy she was.
Whatever cause I might have had, she told him, to hope for your
return, I admit, king's son, that I dared not flatter myself that
you would; and I am usually so unlucky when I long for
something, that this event surprises me. The grateful prince
lavished a thousand caresses on her; he told her of the success of

his trip, of which she knew more perhaps than he, and that the king wanted a piece of cloth that could pass through the eye of a needle; that in truth he thought such a thing impossible, but that he had determined to attempt it, placing all his faith in her friendship and help. White Cat assumed a solemn air, telling him that it was indeed something to ponder seriously, that fortunately there were cats in the castle who were excellent weavers, and that she herself would put her claw to the task and help to further his quest; thus he could set his mind at rest and not think of seeking elsewhere what he would find more easily in her domain than anywhere else in the world.

The hands appeared, bearing torches; and the prince followed them along with White Cat; they entered a magnificent gallery that bordered a great river, over which an immense and astounding display of fireworks was set off. Four cats were to be burned, whose trial had been in due accordance with the law. They were accused of having devoured the roast intended for White Cat's supper, her cheese, her milk; of having gone so far as to conspire against her person with Martafax* and Lhermite,* two famous rats of the region, and named as such by La Fontaine, a most reputable author: but with all that, it was known that there had been a great deal of intrigue in the affair, and that most of the witnesses had been tampered with. However that may be, the prince obtained their pardon. The fireworks harmed no one, and such beautiful sky-rockets have still to be seen again.

A dainty midnight supper was served, which pleased the prince more than the fireworks, for he was very hungry, and his wooden horse had brought him more quickly than any coach could have travelled. The days that followed were like those that had gone before, with a thousand different celebrations that

White Cat devised to amuse her guest. He was perhaps the first mortal to be so well entertained by cats, without any other company.

It is true that White Cat had a pleasant, good-natured and almost omniscient mind. She was more learned than a cat is permitted to be. This surprised the prince sometimes. No, he told her, it's not natural, all the marvellous qualities I behold in you: if you love me, charming puss, tell me by what marvel you think and speak so accurately, that you could easily be received in the most learned academies? Enough of your questions, king's son, she would say; I am not allowed to answer, and you may push your conjectures as far as you like, without my preventing you; let it be enough that for you I shall always keep my claws drawn in, and that I interest myself tenderly in everything that concerns you.

Imperceptibly this second year flowed by like the first; the prince had scarcely to wish for something when the diligent hands would bring it to him then and there, whether it were books, jewels, paintings, antique medals; in fact he had but to say, I want such and such a jewel, that is in the treasury of the Great Mogul or the king of Persia, such and such a statue from Corinth or Greece, for whatever he desired to materialise before him, without his knowing who had brought it nor whence it had come. Such distractions are scarcely wearisome; and when one is in the mood for amusements one is sometimes more than pleased to find oneself master of the most beautiful treasures on earth.

White Cat, who always kept an eye on the prince's interests, advised him that the time for his departure was approaching, that he need not concern himself over the piece of cloth he wished for, and that she had made him a marvellous one; she added that she wished this time to provide him with a retinue worthy of his rank, and, without waiting for his reply, she bade him look down into the great courtyard of the castle. There stood an open barouche made of flame-coloured enamelled gold, with a thousand emblematic figures which pleased the mind as much as the eye. Twelve snow-white horses, four abreast, hauled it, fitted with flame-coloured velvet harnesses embroidered with diamonds and embellished with gold plaques. The barouche was similarly upholstered inside, and a hundred coaches with eight horses, crowded with noblemen of superb mien, magnificently clad, followed the barouche. It was further accompanied by a thousand footsoldiers whose uniforms were so densely embroidered that the cloth could not be seen underneath. What was singular was that wherever one looked, one saw the portrait of White Cat, whether in the emblems of the barouche or on the footsoldiers' uniforms, or attached with a ribbon to the jerkins of those who completed the procession, like a new order of merit that had just been bestowed on them.

Go, she told the prince, go and make your appearance at the court of the king your father, in a manner so sumptuous that your lordly air will sway him, so that he may no longer refuse you the crown you deserve. Here is a walnut; make sure you break it only when you are in his presence; you'll find therein the piece of cloth you asked me for. Adorable Blanchette, he said to her, I confess that I am so saturated with your kindnesses, that if you cared to consent, I would prefer spending my life with you to all the grandeurs that I have reason to anticipate elsewhere. King's son, she replied, I am persuaded of your goodness of heart, it is a rare piece of merchandise among princes, they want to be loved by everyone and to love nothing; but you are proof that the general rule has its exception. I take note of the attachment you display for a little White Cat, who is by nature good for nothing but catching mice. The prince kissed her paw, and left.

One could scarcely believe the speed at which he travelled, did we not already know how the wooden horse had borne him in less than two days more than five hundred leagues from the castle; the same power that animated the horse urged the others on so relentlessly that they took but twenty-four hours to make the journey; they made no halt until they reached the king's domain, where the prince's two elder brothers had already arrived; they, noting that the young prince still hadn't appeared, congratulated themselves on his negligence and muttered to each other: Here is good news; he's dead or sick, and won't be our rival in the important matter we have come to settle. Thereupon they unfolded their cloths, which in truth were so fine that they passed through the eye of a large needle, but not through that of a small one; and the king, greatly relieved by this pretext for a squabble, showed them the needle he had proposed, and which the magistrates, following his orders, had brought from the city treasury where it had been carefully locked up.

There was much murmuring over this dispute. The princes' friends, and especially those of the elder, for his cloth was the more beautiful, argued that this was a piece of outright chicanery, into which much pettifoggery and hair-splitting had entered. The king's supporters maintained that he was scarcely obliged to hold to conditions which he hadn't proposed; finally, to settle all their bickering, a charming sound of trumpets, oboes and kettledrums was heard; it was our prince arriving in pomp with all his retinue. The king and his two sons were all equally amazed by such splendour.

After he had respectfully greeted his father and embraced his brothers, he withdrew the walnut from a ruby-encrusted casket and cracked it open; he supposed he would find the much vaunted piece of cloth within, but instead there was a hazelnut. He cracked again and was amazed to find a cherry stone. Everyone exchanged glances, the king was laughing quietly and thought his son a ninny for having the naïveté to think that he could transport a piece of cloth in a walnut, yet why wouldn't he think so, since he had already brought him a little dog that fitted inside an acorn? Accordingly he cracked the cherry stone, which had a solid kernel; at that an uproar broke out in the chamber, everyone was saying that the prince had been duped in his adventure. He replied nothing to the courtiers' malicious pleasantries; he opened the kernel and found a grain of wheat and inside that a millet seed. Ha! Now it was his turn to be suspicious, and he muttered between his teeth: White Cat, White Cat, you have tricked me. At that moment he felt a cat's claw on his hand, which scratched him so forcefully that his hand bled. He couldn't decide whether this scratch was meant to encourage him or make him lose heart. Nevertheless he pried open the millet seed, and great was the astonishment of all when he withdrew from it a piece of linen four hundred ells long, of such extraordinary stitchery that all the birds, animals and fish were depicted on it, along with the plants of the earth, its rocky peaks, the curiosities and shellfish of the sea, the sun, the moon, the stars, the heavenly bodies and planets of the heavens; as well as the portraits of the kings and other sovereigns who reigned on earth at that time; those of their wives, their mistresses, their children and all their subjects, down to the last street urchin. Each one according to his condition was portrayed with the character that suited him, and was dressed according to the fashion of his native land. When the king saw the piece of linen he grew pale as the prince had blushed red while he was searching so long for it. The needle was presented, and the cloth was passed and repassed through it six times. The king and the two princes maintained a gloomy silence, even though the beauty and rarity of the piece of linen forced them to acknowledge from time to time that everything else in the universe was inferior to it.

The king heaved a deep sigh, and, turning toward his sons, said: Nothing can console me in my old age as much as the spectacle of your deference to my wishes; therefore I wish to put you to one more test. Go once more on a year-long journey, and whoever returns at the end of the year with the most beautiful maiden shall wed her and be crowned king on his marriage; it is of course imperative that my successor have a wife. I swear and promise that I shall no longer postpone the recompense I have offered.

The injustice of all this stunned our prince. The little dog and the linen cloth were worth ten kingdoms rather than one; but he was so well bred that he in no way wished to oppose his father's will, and, without hesitation, climbed back into his barouche; all his retinue followed, and he returned to his beloved White Cat; she knew the day and the moment he would arrive; the road was strewn with flowers, and a thousand incense-burners were smoking on every side, and especially within the castle. She was seated on a Persian carpet, beneath a tent made of cloth-of-gold, in a loggia from which she could see him approaching. He was received by the hands which had always served him. All the cats climbed up to the eaves, so as to congratulate him with a desperate caterwauling.

How now, king's son, she said to him, so you have returned without a crown? Madam, he replied, your favours would indeed have gained it for me; but I am persuaded that the king's distress at parting with it would be greater than my pleasure in possessing it. No matter, she said, you must neglect nothing to deserve it; I will serve you on this occasion; and since you must lead a beautiful maiden back to your father's court, I'll look for one who will win you the prize. Meanwhile, let's rejoice; I have ordained a naval battle between my cats and the terrible rats that infest the region. My cats will be at a disadvantage, perhaps, for they are afraid of the water; but otherwise their superiority would be too great, and one must, insofar as possible, let equality reign in all things. The prince admired the probity of Madam Kitty. He sang her praises, and accompanied her on to a terrace which looked toward the sea.

The cats' vessels consisted of large chunks of cork, on which they sailed along quite easily. The rats had joined together several egg shells, and these were their warships. The combat was cruelly unsparing; the rats dived into the water, and swam much better than the cats, so that the latter were twenty times victors and vanquished; but Minagrobis, admiral of the feline fleet, pursued the rattish hordes to their ultimate débâcle. He devoured the general of their navy with his sharp teeth; it was an old, battle-scarred rat who had gone thrice around the world in stout vessels, wherein he was neither captain nor sailor, but merely an uninvited scrounger.

White Cat did not desire the total destruction of these unfortunates. Well versed in politics, she understood that if there were neither rats nor mice in the land, her subjects would lapse into a state of idleness which might be detrimental to their well-being. The prince spent this year doing what he had done in the preceding ones, that is to say in hunting, fishing and gaming, for White Cat was an excellent chess player. From time to time he couldn't resist plying her with new questions, so as to know by what miracle she was able to speak. He asked her if she was a fairy, or whether someone had transformed her into a cat; but as she never said anything but what she wished to say, neither did she answer anything but what she wished to answer, which were random words signifying nothing, so that he had no trouble concluding that she didn't choose to share her secret with him.

Nothing flows faster than days that pass without care and without chagrin, and if the Cat hadn't been so careful to remember the time for his return to the court, it is certain that the prince would have forgotten it absolutely. She advised him on the eve that it was only up to him to carry away one of the most beautiful princesses in the world, that the hour to destroy the fairies' fatal handiwork had at last arrived, and that he must resolve to cut off her head and tail and throw them immediately into the fire. Me! he exclaimed. Blanchette! My love! Me, a barbarian who would slay you! Ah, no doubt you wish to put my heart to the test, but rest assured that it is incapable of lacking in the love and gratitude it owes you. No, king's son, she continued, I suspect you of no ingratitude; I know your worth; neither you nor I may control our destiny in this affair. Do as I wish and we shall each of us begin to know happiness, and you will understand, on my honour as a cat, that I am truly your friend.

Tears came two or three times to the eyes of the young prince, at the mere thought that he must cut off the head of his little pussycat who was so graceful and pretty. Again he said everything he could think of to dissuade her; she replied obstinately that she wished to die at his hand; and that it was the only way to prevent his brothers from assuming the crown; in a word she urged him with such ardour, that trembling, he drew his sword and with an unsteady hand cut off the head and tail of his good friend the Cat; at the same moment he witnessed the most charming metamorphosis imaginable. White Cat's body grew tall, and suddenly changed into a girl. It would be impossible to describe how perfect she was in every detail, how superior to all other maidens. Her eyes delighted all hearts, and her sweetness gave them pause: her form was regal, her manner noble and modest, her nature affectionate, her manners engaging; in a word, she towered above all that was most lovable in the world.

Seeing her, the prince was overcome with surprise, a surprise so delightful that he thought he must be under a spell. He was unable to speak; his eyes weren't big enough to look at her; he was too tongue-tied to explain his amazement, but even this paled when he saw an enormous crowd of ladies and lords enter the room, each with their cat's skin slung over their shoulders: they knelt before the queen and expressed their joy at seeing her again in her natural state. She received them with tokens of kindness which bore ample witness to the goodness of her heart. And after holding court for a few moments, she ordered that she be left alone with the prince, and addressed him thus: Do not imagine, my lord, that I was always a Cat, nor that my condition among men was a lowly one. My father was the ruler of six kingdoms. He loved my mother tenderly, and gave her absolute freedom to do as she wished. Her chief passion was for travel, and so it came about that while she was carrying me she undertook to go and see a certain mountain, of which she had heard tell surprising things. As she was on her way there, she was told that close to the place she was passing through was a fairy's ancient castle, the most beautiful in the world, or at any rate so it was supposed to be, according to legend, for since no one ever entered there, no one could be sure; but what was known with certainty was that in their garden those fairies had the finest fruits, the tastiest and most delicate that ever were eaten.

Immediately my mother the queen had such a violent urge to taste them that she made straight for the castle. She arrived at the gate of that magnificent edifice, which glittered with gold and lapis on all sides, but she knocked to no avail; no one at all appeared; it seemed that everyone inside was dead. Her appetite whetted by frustration, she called for ladders to be brought so that she might climb over the walls into the garden; and this would have happened, but the walls grew taller before their very eyes, even though nobody was seen at work on them; ladders were joined together; they collapsed under the weight of those ordered to climb them, who were injured or killed.

The queen was in despair. She saw great trees laden with fruits which she imagined to be delicious, she would eat of them or die; thus she had gorgeous tents pitched before the castle, and remained there six weeks with all her court. She neither ate nor slept, but sighed unceasingly; she spoke of naught but the fruits of the inaccessible garden; at last she fell dangerously ill, without anyone's being able to supply her with the slightest remedy, for the inexorable fairies hadn't even made an appearance since she installed herself near their castle. Her officers were all deeply distressed: one heard nothing but sobs and sighs, while the dying queen demanded fruits of those who served her, but would have only those that were denied her.

One night when she had dozed off a bit, she saw on waking a little old woman, ugly and decrepit, seated in an armchair by her bedside. She was surprised that her ladies-in-waiting would have let a stranger come so close, when the woman said: We find your majesty most importunate, to wish so obstinately to eat of our fruits; but since your precious life hangs in the balance, my sisters and I have consented to give you as much as you can carry with you, and for as long as you stay here, provided you make us a gift. Ah! good mother, speak, I'll give you my kingdoms, my heart, my soul, if only I may have fruits; I couldn't pay them too dear! We wish, she said, that your majesty give us the daughter you are carrying in your womb; as soon as she is born, we shall come to fetch her; she will be well cared for with us, there are no virtues, no beauties, no sciences with which we shan't endow her: in a word, she will be our child, we shall make her happy; but note that your majesty will not see her again until she be wed. If this proposal suits you I shall cure you straight away, and lead you to our orchards; in spite of the night you will see clear enough to choose what you like. If what I tell you displeases you, good evening, your highness the queen, I am going to sleep. However harsh the law you impose upon me, replied the queen, I accept it rather than perish; for it is certain that I haven't a day left to live, thus I shall lose my child in losing myself. Heal me, wise fairy, she went on, and let me not wait a moment before savouring the privilege you have just granted me.

The fairy touched her with a little gold wand, saying: May your majesty be free of all the ills which bind you to this bed. At once it seemed to her that a harsh and heavy cloak that had been crushing her was lifted from her shoulders, and that there were places where she felt it still. It was apparently these places where the evil was the most severe. She had her ladies summoned, and gaily told them how well she felt, that she was going to rise from her bed, and that at last the fairies' palace gates, so strongly bolted and barricaded, were to be opened for her to eat the lovely fruits, and take away as many as she pleased.

All of her ladies-in-waiting supposed that the queen was raving, and that at this moment she was dreaming of the fruits she had so longed for; so that instead of replying they began to weep, and had the physicians awakened so they could see the state she was in. This delay drove the queen to despair; she at once demanded her robes; they were refused her; she grew angry, her face reddened. They said it was because of the fever; but now the doctors arrived and, after they had taken her pulse and performed their usual rigmarole, were obliged to admit that she was in perfect health. Her ladies, realising the error their zeal had caused them to commit, sought to repair it and lost no time in dressing her. Each begged her pardon, the matter was settled, and she hastened to follow the old fairy who was still awaiting her.

She entered the palace, where nothing could have been added to make it the most beautiful place in the world; you will believe it easily, my lord, added Queen White Cat, when I tell you that it's the very one in which we are at this moment; two other fairies a little less aged than the one who led my mother met them at the gate, and welcomed her most kindly. She beseeched them to lead her directly to the garden, and towards the espaliers where the finest fruits were to be found. All are equally good, they replied, and if it weren't for your wanting to have the pleasure of plucking them yourself, we should have only to call out for them to arrive here. I beg you, ladies, to let me have the satisfaction of seeing such an extraordinary sight. The oldest stuck her fingers in her mouth and whistled three times; then called out: Apricots, peaches, clingstones, nectarines, cherries, plums, white cherries, melons, pears, muscats, apples, oranges, lemons, currants, strawberries, raspberries, come when I call! But, said the queen, all those you have just called for ripen in different seasons. That is not the case with our orchards, they told her; we have all the fruits that exist on earth, always ripe, always good, and they never spoil.

And at that very moment they arrived, rolling, creeping, pell-mell, without getting bruised or dirty; in such wise that the queen, anxious to slake her craving, flung herself on them, seized the first that came to her hands, and devoured rather than ate them.

Feeling a little sated now, she begged the fairies to let her go and see the espaliers, so as to have the pleasure of inspecting them before making her choice. We are happy to let you, said the three fairies, but remember the promise you gave us; you will no longer be allowed to retract it. I am persuaded, she replied, that life here with you is so agreeable, and this palace seems so fine to me, that were it not for the love I bear my husband the king, I would offer to remain here; for this reason you must never believe that I would take back my word. The fairies, delighted, opened all their gardens and enclosures to her; she stayed for three days and three nights without wishing to leave, so delicious did she find everything. She gathered fruits for her provision, and since they never spoil, she had four thousand mules brought to her and laden with them. The fairies added gold baskets of exquisite workmanship to hold them, and several rarities whose price was excessive; they promised to raise me as a princess, to make me perfect, and to choose me a husband; that she would be notified of the wedding and that they sincerely hoped she would attend.

The king was delighted by the queen's return; the whole court bore witness to his joy; there were balls, masquerades, tilting at the ring,* and feasts at which the queen's fruits were served as a sumptuous treat. The king ate them in preference to everything that was served him. He knew nothing of the bargain she had struck with the fairies, and often asked her in what country she had found such goodies; she replied that they came from an almost inaccessible mountain; another time she said they came from valleys, and then from a garden in the depths of a vast forest. The king was surprised by so many contradictions. He questioned those who accompanied her, but she had so sternly forbidden them to tell anyone of her adventure, that they dared not speak of it. Finally, disturbed by what she had promised the fairies, and sensing the time of her confinement fast approaching, she sank into a frightful state of despondency, so that even her appearance was altered. The king was distressed, and urged the queen to tell him the cause of her sadness, and after much shedding of tears, she told him everything that had happened between herself and the fairies, and how she had promised them the child she was expecting. What! cried the king, we have no offspring, you know how much I long for a child, and for a matter of two or three apples you are capable of giving yours away? Obviously you love me not at all. Thereupon he overwhelmed her with a thousand reproaches, causing my poor mother to feel she would die of grief, but not content with this, he had her shut up in a tower with guards on all sides to prevent her from having commerce with anyone in the outside world, save the officers who waited on her, and even so he removed those who had been with her to the fairies' castle.

The bad blood between the king and queen plunged the court into deep consternation. Everyone doffed their rich robes to dress in a manner more suited to the general sorrow. The king, for his part, appeared inexorable; he no longer saw his wife, and as soon as I was born he had me brought to his palace to be nursed, while she remained a prisoner and crushed by misery. The fairies were ignorant of nothing that had happened; they grew irritated, they wanted me, they considered me their property and that they had been robbed of it. Before mapping a vengeance which would be proportionate to the crime, they sent an illustrious embassy to the king, warning him to release the queen and restore her to favour, and to beg him also to hand me over to their ambassadors so that I might be raised and educated by them. The ambassadors were so stunted and so deformed, for they were in fact hideous dwarfs, that they were in no way able to persuade the king to do their bidding. He refused them rudely, and if they hadn't left post-haste they might have met with a worse fate.

When the fairies learned of my father's actions, their indignation knew no bounds; and after dispatching into his six kingdoms all the ills that could render them desolate, they unleashed a horrendous dragon who scattered venom wherever he passed, devoured grown men and children, and with his breath caused trees and plants to die.

The king was sunk in the deepest despair; he consulted all the sages in his realm to learn what he should do to protect his subjects from the misfortunes in which he saw them engulfed. They advised him to seek throughout the world for the finest doctors and the surest remedies, and, on the other hand, to release criminals condemned to die so that they might combat the dragon. Quite satisfied with this opinion, the king acted on it but received no consolation, for the death toll continued to grow, and no one could approach the dragon without being devoured, so that at last he had recourse to a fairy who had protected him from his earliest childhood. She was very old, and scarcely ever left her bed any more; he betook himself to her dwelling and reproached her a thousand times for having let destiny persecute him without coming to his aid. What do you want me to do, she said, you have annoyed my sisters; they have as much power as I, and it is very rarely that we act against each other. Think of appeasing them by giving them your daughter, that little princess belongs to them. You have shut up the queen in a prison cell:

what has that lovable woman done to you for you to treat her thus? Decide then to keep the word she gave, and I guarantee that you will be showered with blessings.

The king my father loved me dearly, but seeing no other way to save his kingdoms and be rid of the fatal dragon, he told his old friend that he had resolved to believe her, that he would agree to hand me over to the fairies, since she assured him I would be cherished and raised as a princess of my rank; that he would also send for the queen, and that the old fairy had only to tell him to whom he should deliver me to have me brought to the fairies' castle. She replied that I must be carried in my cradle to the top of the mountain of flowers; you may even stay in the region, she said, to be a spectator of the celebration that will be held there. The king told her he would go there in a week's time with the queen, and that she should notify her sister fairies, so that they might do whatever might seem fitting to them.

No sooner had he returned to the palace when he had the queen summoned with a tenderness and pomp equal to the wrath and fury with which he had her made prisoner. She was so changed and dejected that he could scarcely recognise her, had not his heart assured him that this was the same person he had loved so much. With tears in his eyes he begged her to forget the grief he had caused her, assuring her that it would be the last she would ever suffer on his account. She replied that she had brought it on herself through the imprudence of promising her child to the fairies; and if anything could plead in her behalf, it was the state she was in; at last he informed her that he would place me in their hands. The queen in turn fought against this proposal; it seemed that some fatality must have been in all this, and that I would always be an object of discord between my father and my mother. After she had wept and moaned for a long time, without his granting her wish (for the king saw only too well the tragic consequences, and that his subjects would continue to die, as though it were they who had brought misfortune on our family), she agreed to everything he wanted, and preparations for the ceremony began.

I was placed in a cradle made of mother-of-pearl, ornamented with as much elegance as art can summon. Garlands of flowers and festoons hung round it, and the flowers were precious stones of different colours which flashed so brightly when the sun struck them that one had to look away. The magnificence of my costume surpassed, if it is possible, that of the cradle. My swaddling bands were made of enormous pearls; twenty-four princesses of the blood carried me on a sort of finely wrought litter; their robes were unmatched, but they were allowed to wear no other colour but white, in keeping with my innocence. The whole court accompanied me, each according to his rank.

As we all started up the mountain, a melodious orchestra was heard approaching; at last the fairies appeared, thirty-six in all; they had invited their closest lady-friends to accompany them; each was seated in a shell of pearl, larger than the one on which Venus emerged from the sea; sea-horses, which travel with difficulty on land, drew them in their chariots; they acted more pompous than the greatest queens in the universe, but were in fact exceeding old and ugly. They brought an olive branch, to show the king that his submission found favour with them; and when they held me, they caressed me so fondly that it seemed they longer wished to live with any goal but that of making me happy.

The dragon which they had employed to avenge themselves on my father followed behind them, bound with diamond chains; they held me in their arms, bestowed a thousand caresses on me, and endowed me with numerous advantages; then began the fairies' dance. It was a sprightly one indeed; and it was amazing to see these old ladies hop and gambol. Then the dragon who had devoured so many people approached. The three fairies to whom my mother had promised me perched on him with my cradle between them; he spread his enormous scaly wings, finer than crêpe and shot through with a thousand bizarre colours, and thus we travelled back to the castle. My mother, seeing me in the air, exposed on the back of that furious dragon, couldn't prevent herself from uttering several piercing cries. The king consoled her, reminding her of the promise his friend had given that no harm would befall me and that they would take as good care of me as I would receive in his own palace. She calmed herself, even though it was most painful for her to contemplate losing me for so long, and to be the only cause of it; for if she hadn't desired to eat the fruits in that garden, I would have remained in the kingdom of the king my father, and would not have had to endure all the sorrows that I have still to recount to you.

Know then, king's son, that my guardians had had a tower built expressly for me, in which there were a thousand handsome apartments for all the seasons of the year, magnificent furniture, delightful books, but no door: one could enter only through the windows, which were prodigiously high. There was a lovely garden on top of the tower, decked with flowers, fountains and nooks of greenery which protected one from the heat of the most scorching dog-days. It was here that the fairies brought me up with attentions that surpassed all that they had promised the queen. My clothes were of the latest fashion, and so magnificent that, seeing me, one would have thought it were my wedding day. They taught me everything suitable to my age and rank; I gave them very little trouble, for I learned almost everything with great facility; they found my gentle temperament most agreeable, and since I had never seen anyone but them, I might have stayed quietly in this situation for the rest of my life.

They always came to visit me astride the furious dragon of whom I have already told; they never spoke to me of the king or the queen; they called me their daughter, and I thought I was. Not a soul lived with me in the tower, except for a parrot and a little dog, that they gave me for my playmates, for they had the gift of reason and were marvellously well spoken.

One side of the tower was built alongside a sunken road, so encumbered with trees and ruts that I had never seen anyone on it since they had confined me there. But one day, as I was at the window chatting with my parrot and my dog, I heard a noise. Looking around I perceived a young knight who had stopped to listen to our conversation; I had never before seen a man except in pictures. I was by no means vexed that a chance encounter provided me with this opportunity, so that, not fearing in the least the danger that comes with the satisfaction of seeing an amiable object, I drew closer to look at him, and the more I looked at him, the more pleasure I experienced. He made me a deep bow and fixed his gaze on me, seeming at a loss how to converse with me, for my window was so high up that he feared being overheard, and he well knew that I was in the fairies' castle.

Suddenly, night fell; or rather, it arrived without our noticing; he blew two or three times on his horn, and delighted me with several fanfares, then he left without my being able to discern even the direction he took, so thick was the darkness. I remained plunged in a waking dream; I no longer experienced the same pleasure in chatting with my parrot and my dog. They recounted me the most delightful things imaginable, for fairy animals become very witty, but my thoughts were elsewhere, and I hadn't learned the art of controlling myself. Sinbad the parrot noticed this, for he was clever, and didn't mention what was on his mind.*

I didn't fail to arise at daybreak. I ran to my window, and was agreeably surprised to find the young knight at the foot of the tower. He was sumptuously clad, and I flattered myself that I was partly the cause, nor was I mistaken. He spoke to me through a kind of trumpet which carried his voice up to me, and by this means he told me that, having been indifferent until now to all the beautiful women he had seen, he suddenly felt so powerfully stricken with me that he couldn't live unless he were to see me every day of his life. I was highly pleased by this compliment, and most disturbed that I was unable to respond to it, for I should have had to shout at the top of my voice, and put myself in danger of being heard better by the fairies than by him. I was holding a few flowers which I threw down to him; he caught them as though they were a distinguished favour, kissed them several times and tendered me his thanks. Then he asked me if I thought it wise that he come every day at the same time and stand beneath my windows, and that if I did so, to throw him an object of some kind. I had a turquoise ring which I quickly removed from my finger and threw down to him in haste, signalling him to go away as fast as possible, for I had just heard the fairy Violenta on the other side of the tower, who had mounted her dragon to bring me my breakfast.

The first thing she said on entering was: I smell a man's voice here: Dragon, look for him. Ah! I had guessed right! I was terrified that the beast might fly through the other window and follow the knight, in whose fortunes I already took a lively interest. Truly, good mother, I said (for the fairy wished that I address her thus), you are making sport of me. Does a voice smell of something? And if it did, is there a mortal bold enough to venture to climb this tower? You speak truly, child, she replied, and I am delighted to see you reason so prettily; I suppose it must be the hatred I have for all men that sometimes persuades me they can't be far off. She gave me my breakfast and my distaff. When you have eaten you must get back to your spinning, she told me, for you did nothing yesterday, and my sisters will be angry. In truth, I had been so preoccupied with the stranger that it had been impossible for me to spin.

As soon as she left I threw down the distaff with a mutinous little gesture, and climbed up to my terrace to gaze as far off into the countryside as I could. I had an excellent telescope; nothing blocked my view, I peered about on all sides, and discovered my knight at the top of a mountain. He was resting under an opulent tent made of cloth-of-gold, and was attended by a large retinue. I had no doubt that he was the son of some king of the region of the fairies' castle. Since I feared that if he returned to the tower he might be discovered by the terrible dragon, I picked up my parrot and told him to fly as far as the mountain, that he would find the stranger who had spoken to me there, and to beg him on my behalf not to come back again, for I dreaded the vigilance of my guardians, and feared lest they cause him harm.

The parrot fulfilled his assignment with his inborn cleverness. Everyone was surprised to see him flying straight to his destination and perch on the prince's shoulder so as to whisper in his ear. The prince experienced the joy and pain of this embassy. The precautions I had taken for him flattered his heart; but the obstacles that prevented him from speaking with me crushed him, without being able to dissuade him from carrying out the plan he had devised for pleasing me. He asked Sinbad a thousand questions, and Sinbad for his part asked him a hundred others, for he was by nature inquisitive. The king gave him a ring for me in exchange for my turquoise; it too was a turquoise, but much more beautiful than mine; it was carved in a heart-shape and set with diamonds. It is only right for me to treat you as an ambassador, he added: here is my portrait; take it and show it only to your lovely mistress. He fastened the portrait under Sinbad's wing and placed the ring in his beak.

I awaited the return of my little green messenger with an impatience I had never felt before. He told me that he to whom I had dispatched him was a great king, that he had received him as hospitably as could be, that I could be sure that he no longer wished to live except for my sake, and that despite the great peril of coming to the foot of the tower, he was determined to undertake anything rather than renounce seeing me again. This news intrigued me very much, and I started to cry. Sinbad and

Fido consoled me as best they could, for they loved me tenderly; then Sinbad presented me with the prince's ring, and showed me the portrait. I confess I had never been so delighted as I was at being able to contemplate close up him who I had hitherto perceived only from a distance. He seemed even more attractive than before; a hundred thoughts flooded my mind, some agreeable, others sad, giving me an appearance of extreme restlessness. The fairies who came to see me noticed this. They told each other that doubtless I was growing bored, and that it was time to think of finding me a husband of the race of fairies. They mentioned several, and settled on little King Migonnet, whose kingdom lay five hundred thousand leagues from their palace, but that was of scant importance. Sinbad listened to this learned council and came to tell me of it, saying: Ah! how I pity you, dear mistress, if you become Queen Migonnet! He's a frightful-looking scarecrow, I regret to tell you; in truth the king who loves you wouldn't have him as his flunkey. Then you've seen him, Sinbad! I should say I have, he continued; I was brought up on a branch alongside him. What, on a branch? I continued. Yes, he replied, for he has the claws of an eagle.

Such a tale afflicted me strangely; I gazed on the charming portrait of the young king, I esteemed that he had given it to Sinbad only so that I might find a way to see him; and when I compared his face with Migonnet, I no longer hoped for anything from life, and resolved to die rather than marry him.

I slept not a wink all night. Sinbad and Fido chatted with me; towards morning I dozed off a little; and, since my dog had a keen nose, he sensed that the prince was at the front of the tower. He woke Sinbad: I'll wager, he said, that the king is down there. Be still, chatterbox; since you almost always have your eyes open and your ears cocked, you're annoyed when others sleep. But let's wager, brave Fido insisted, I know that he's there. And as for me, I know he's not; haven't I forbidden him to come here on behalf of our noble mistress? Ah, this is too much, you're getting on my nerves with your excuses, cried my dog; a man of passion consults only his heart; and thereupon he began to tug so hard at Sinbad's wings that the parrot grew furious. Their quarrelling awoke me; they told me its cause; I ran or rather flew to the window; I saw the king stretching out his arms to me, telling me with his trumpet that he could no longer live without me, beseeching me to find a way to leave my tower or to let him enter it, that he called on all the gods and the elements to witness that he would marry me at once, and that I would be one of the greatest queens in the universe.

I ordered Sinbad to go and tell him that what he wished seemed all but impossible; that none the less, in view of the promise he had given me and the oaths he had tendered, I would work diligently to help him realise his wishes; that I begged him not to come every day, lest he be finally spied by someone, and that the fairies were pitiless.

He withdrew overcome with joy, thanks to the flattering hopes I held out to him while I found myself in the worst predicament I had ever known, when I reflected on what I had just promised. How could I leave this tower, which had no doors? and with only the help of Sinbad and Fido? And I so young, so inexperienced, so fearful? I therefore resolved not to undertake anything which had no hope of success, and I sent Sinbad to tell the king. He was ready to kill himself before Sinbad's very eyes, but finally he ordered him to persuade me either to come and watch him die, or to comfort him. Sire, cried the winged ambassador, my mistress is sufficiently convinced, she lacks only power.

When he came to tell me all that had happened, I was more afflicted than before. Fairy Violenta arrived; seeing how my eyes were red and swollen, she said that I had wept, and that if I didn't tell her why she would burn me, for all her threats were always terrible. I answered, trembling, that I was tired of spinning, and that I longed to have nets to catch the little birds who came to peck at the fruits in my garden. What you desire shall cost you no more tears, my daughter; I shall bring you all the cords you need; and in fact I received them that very evening; but she cautioned me to think less of work and more about making myself beautiful, since King Migonnet would soon be arriving. I shuddered at this disturbing news, and answered nothing.

As soon as she left I began to work on two or three bits of netting, but my real endeavour was to fashion a rope ladder which would be skilfully made, even though I had never seen one. It is true that the fairy never supplied me with as much cord as I needed, and she kept repeating: But daughter, your weaving is like Penelope's, it never progresses, and you are continually asking me for more supplies. O! Good mother, I said, it's easy enough for you to talk! Can't you see that I'm inexperienced, and that I keep spoiling my work and throwing it into the fire? Are you afraid of my impoverishing you with my string? My simple airs delighted her, even though she had a most disagreeable and cruel nature.

I dispatched Sinbad to tell the king to come one evening beneath the tower windows, that he would find a ladder there, and that he would find out the rest when he came. As a matter of fact I anchored it firmly, resolved to flee with him; but when he saw it he climbed it in haste, without waiting for me to come down, and burst into my chamber while I was preparing everything for my flight.

The sight of him so filled me with joy that I forgot the peril both of us were in. He renewed his gallant vows, and beseeched me to delay no longer in accepting him as my husband; we enlisted Sinbad and Fido as witnesses of our marriage; never was a wedding between persons of such high rank celebrated with less noise and festivity, and never were hearts happier than ours.

Day had not yet come when the king left me: I told him the fairies' frightful plan of marrying me to little Migonnet; I described his face, which horrified him as much as me. Hardly had he left when the hours began to seem like days; I ran to the window and followed him with my gaze despite the darkness; but what was my amazement on seeing in the distance a chariot of fire drawn by winged salamanders, travelling with such speed that the eye could scarcely follow it! The chariot was escorted by a quantity of guards mounted on ostriches. I had barely time enough to glance at the ugly sprite who was travelling through the air in this fashion; but I concluded at once that it was a fairy or an enchanter.

Soon after, fairy Violenta entered my chamber: I bring you good news, she said; your lover arrived a few hours ago; prepare to receive him; here are some jewels and finery. What! I cried out. And who told you I wished to be wed? It's not my intention at all; send King Migonnet back where he came from; I won't add so much as a pin to my dress; let him find me beautiful or ugly, it's all the same to me. Ah, ah, replied the fairy, such a little rebel, such a hare-brain! I'm in no mood for jokes, and I'm going to . . . You'll do what to me? I retorted, blushing at the names she had called me. Can one be more dismally treated than I, shut up in a tower with a parrot and a dog, having to look several times a day at the frightful face of a dragon? Ha! Ungrateful wretch, said the fairy, and what did you do to deserve so much care and trouble on the part of others? I've said it all too often to my sisters, that we shall have but a sad recompense. She went to find them and tell them of our quarrel, and all were equally shocked.

Sinbad and Fido pleaded desperately with me, saying that if I continued in my refractory ways, they foresaw that harsh treatment would be visited on me. I felt so proud at possessing the heart of a great king that I scorned the fairies and the advice of my little friends. I refused to don my finery, and purposely coiffed my hair awry, so that Migonnet might find me displeasing. Our interview took place on the terrace. He arrived in his chariot of fire. Never since there were dwarfs was such a tiny one to be seen. He walked on his eagle's claws and his knees at the same time, for there were no bones in his legs, so that he was obliged to support himself on two diamond crutches. His royal robe was only half an ell long, and a third of it trailed on the ground. His head was as big as a bushel basket, and his nose so large that a dozen birds perched on it, whose chirping delighted him; he had such an enormous beard that canaries had made their nests in it, and his ears over-topped his head by a cubit, but this was scarcely noticeable thanks to the high pointed crown that he wore so as to appear taller. The flame of his chariot roasted the fruits, withered the flowers, and dried up the fountains of my garden. He approached me with open arms to embrace me; I stood up straight, and his first equerry was obliged to lift him; but as soon as he drew near I fled into my chamber and slammed shut the door and the windows, so that Migonnet returned to the fairies' abode extremely vexed with me.

They asked him a thousand pardons for my brusqueness, and to calm him, for he was very powerful, they resolved to lead him into my chamber at night while I was asleep, to bind my hands and feet and put me with him in the burning chariot, so that he might carry me away. Once this plan was agreed on, they hardly even scolded me for my insolent behaviour. All they said was that I should think about making amends. Sinbad and Fido were surprised at such mildness. You know, mistress, said my dog, my heart tells me no good can come of this. My ladies the fairies are strange personages, especially Violenta. I made fun of his warnings, and awaited my beloved husband with wild impatience. He himself was too impatient to put off seeing me again; I threw down the rope ladder, fully resolved to run off with him; he climbed it nimbly and proffered me such tender words that I still dare not summon them to memory.

While we were speaking together with the same tranquillity we would have had in his palace, the windows of my chamber were suddenly battered in. In came the fairies on their terrible dragon, followed by Migonnet in his fiery chariot and all his guards on their ostriches. The king, fearless, put his hand to his sword, thinking only of saving me from the most horrible misadventure that ever was, for, would you believe it, my lord? those barbarous creatures unleashed their dragon on him; he was eaten up before my very eyes.

In desperation at his fate and mine, I threw myself into the jaws of that hideous monster, hoping he would swallow me, as he had just swallowed all that I loved in the world. He would have liked to, but the fairies, even more cruel than he, wouldn't let him. She must be kept for more lingering torments, they screamed; a speedy death is too gentle for this shameless creature! They laid hands on me; at once I saw myself turn into the White Cat; they brought me to this magnificent palace of my father and metamorphosed all the lords and ladies of the kingdom into cats; they spared those whose hands alone would remain visible, and reduced me to the deplorable state in which you found me, informing me of my birth, of the death of my father and of my mother, and that I would never be released from my feline condition, save by a prince who would perfectly resemble the husband they had torn from me. 'Tis you, my lord, who possess that resemblance, she continued: the same features, same aspect, even the same voice; I was struck by it the moment I saw you; I was informed of everything that would happen, and I know as well what will happen: my torment will end. And my own, lovely queen, said the prince, throwing himself at her feet, will it be of long duration? Already I love you more than life itself, my lord, said the queen. We must go to see your father; we shall judge of his feelings for me, and learn if he will consent to what you desire.

She went out; the prince gave her his hand, she mounted into a chariot with him; it was far more magnificent than those he had had before. The rest of the cortège matched it to such a degree that all the horseshoes were made of emeralds, and their nails were diamonds. Perhaps it was a sight never seen before or since. I pass over the agreeable conversations that the queen and the prince were having; if she was matchless in beauty, she was not less so for her mind, and the young prince was as perfect as she, so that they thought only of charming things.

When they were near the castle where the brothers were to

meet, the queen entered a rock crystal whose facets were adorned with gold and rubies. Its interior was curtained so that none could see her, and it was borne by beautifully formed and superbly clad youths. The prince remained in the chariot, from which he saw his brothers strolling with princesses of extraordinary beauty. As soon as they recognised him they asked him if he had brought a fiancée; he told them that he had been so unlucky that throughout his travels he had encountered only ugly women, and that the only thing of rarity he could find to bring was a little White Cat. They began to laugh at his innocence. A cat, they said, are you afraid the mice will eat our palace? The prince replied that in effect it wasn't wise to offer such a present to his father; thereupon they set out on the road to the city.

The elder princes rode with their princesses in barouches made of gold and lapis lazuli; their horses' heads were adorned with plumes and aigrettes; in short, nothing on earth could surpass this brilliant cavalcade. Our young prince followed behind, then came the rock crystal, which everyone stared at admiringly.

The courtiers hastened to tell the king that the three princes were arriving: Have they brought beautiful ladies with them? he retorted. It would be impossible to find anything that could outshine them. This reply seemed to annoy him. The king greeted them cordially, and couldn't decide on whom to bestow the prize; he looked at the youngest and said: So, this time you have come alone? Your majesty will find inside this rock crystal a little White Cat, who miaows so sweetly, and draws in her claws so nicely, that your majesty will surely approve of her. The king smiled, and was about to open the crystal himself, but no sooner had he approached it than the queen, using a spring, caused the whole thing to fall in shards, and appeared like the sun after it has been for some time veiled in clouds; her blonde hair cascaded over her shoulders and fell in thick ringlets down to her feet; her head was wreathed in flowers, her fragile white gauze gown was lined with pink taffeta; she arose and made a deep curtsey before the king, who, overcome with admiration, couldn't prevent himself from crying out: Here is the incomparable one, and it is she who deserves the crown.

Your highness, she replied, I haven't come here to deprive you of a throne which you occupy with so much dignity; I was born with six kingdoms; allow me to offer you one of them, and one to both of your sons. All I ask for in recompense is your friendship, and this young prince for my husband. We shall still be well provided for with three kingdoms. The king and all the court uttered long shouts of joy and astonishment. The marriage was celebrated at once, and those of the two princes as well, in such wise that the whole court spent several months in pleasures and diversions. Each then left to govern his realm; the lovely White Cat was immortalised, as much for her kindness and generosity as for her rare merit and her beauty.

> This young prince was lucky indeed
> To find in a cat's guise an august princess
> Whom he would later marry, and accede
> To three thrones and a world of tenderness.
> When two enchanting eyes are inclined
> To inspire love, they seldom find resistance,
> Especially when a wise and ardent mind
> Moves them to inspire lasting allegiance.

I'll speak no more of the unworthy mother
Who caused the White Cat so many sorrows
By coveting the accursed fruits of another,
Thus ceding her daughter to the fairies' powers.
Mothers, who have children full of charm,
Despise her conduct, and keep them from all harm.

He led the princesses off to a
tower that stood high and lonely
in the palace grounds.

✷ *The Subtle Princess*

Translated by Gilbert Adair

MARIE-JEANNE L'HÉRITIER DE VILLANDON

In the time of the first Crusades, a certain king (as to where his kingdom lay I know no more than that it was in Europe) resolved to make war against the infidels in Palestine. Before undertaking a journey that promised to be long and perilous, he put the affairs of his kingdom in order, and appointed his ablest minister as regent, so that he might feel entirely easy on that account.

What did concern this king, however, was the welfare of his own family. The queen had died, alas, not long before our story properly begins. She had left him no son, but three young princesses, all of marriageable age. My knowledge of the family doesn't extend to their true names: I only know that, in those honest, uncomplicated times, it was the custom among ordinary folk to refer to eminent persons by nicknames chosen according to their good and bad qualities, a custom all the more appropriate to the princesses in that each was so very different from her two sisters it was as if the king had three only children. Thus the eldest of them they nicknamed Lackadaisy; the second, Loquatia; and the last, Finessa; all of which names served, as you'll see, as a witty commentary on the characters of the three sisters.

Never was anyone born who was as lazy as Lackadaisy. She would wake up every day at the same hour, one in the afternoon; would be dragged off to church in much the same condition as when she was dragged out of bed, her hair dishevelled, her gown hanging loose and unfastened, her girdle missing; and would frequently find herself wearing one slipper belonging to one pair and another to another. These lapses would usually be rectified before night, but no one could ever prevail upon her to go other than in slippers: she found the wearing of shoes unutterably fatiguing. As soon as she had dined, she would sit down at her dressing-table and might happily remain there all evening. The rest of her time, till midnight, was spent at play, and at supper. After which, it took as long to peel off her clothes as it had taken to put them on; and she could never be persuaded to go to bed until it was broad daylight outside.

Loquatia led quite another sort of life. Unlike her sister this princess was very brisk and active, and spent next to no time fussing over her appearance. But she had such a frantic itch to talk that, from the instant she awoke till the moment she fell asleep again, her lips were never at rest. Poor Loquatia, she was a mouth without a head. She knew all about everything: what had happened once upon a time and to whom; which couples were living in connubial harmony and which were not; the intrigues and gallantries not only of the court but of the commonest of commoners. She kept a thick register of all those wives of her acquaintance who scrimped at home in order to shine abroad, and knew, down to the very last sou, what the Marquis So-and-So paid his valet and the Countess Such-and-Such her lady-in-waiting. The better, moreover, to keep abreast of such trivial news, she would shamelessly pump her nurse and her dressmaker and listen to all their scandal as solemnly as if she were listening to some ambassador just returned from the Orient; and, believing firmly that people who can't keep their own secrets really shouldn't expect you to keep theirs either, she would instantly repeat everything she heard to everyone she knew, from the king himself to the humblest of his footmen. For, provided she could talk, she little cared who it was she talked to.

This itch of Loquatia to talk, talk, talk, all day long, ended by having a rather unfortunate effect on her reputation. Notwithstanding her high rank, her over-familiar manners emboldened a few of the court's brighter sparks to make love to her, by word if not by act. If she listened, inattentively enough, to their fine and flowery speeches, it was – not unlike those people whose sole gratification in writing a letter is that of receiving a reply – purely to have the pleasure of answering them; for, from morning till night, at whatever cost to the chores and duties that might naturally be expected of her, she lived only to hear others tattle or to tattle away herself. Never did Loquatia, any more than her nonchalant sister, employ herself in thinking, in working or in reading. She never troubled herself with household matters or the amusements of her spindle or needle. In short, like Lackadaisy, she led a life of complete idleness, idleness of mind as well as of body.

The youngest of these three princesses (Reader, it was ever thus) was of a wholly different character. *Her* thoughts and hands were never idle. She was of a surprising vivacity and she applied it only to good use. She danced, sang and played music to perfection. She would finish, with quite wonderful skill, all the finicky little tasks of the hand which are reputed to divert those of her sex; and, when she spoke, it was with the measured caution of a chess player making a move. She oversaw the king's household; and, once and for all, by care and vigilance, put an end to the petty pilferings of his lower officers; for, even in days as halcyon as those, the cheating of princes was rife.

Nor is that anything like a complete inventory of her talents. She deployed in the cause of truth and candour all those wiles, charms and subterfuges that have immemorially been placed at the service of duplicity; and such was her good judgement of things, such was her presence of mind, she never failed to find the means of extricating those dear to her from the greatest difficulties. Young as she was, for instance, she had cleverly discovered, in a treaty that was just about to be signed, that a perfidious foreign ambassador had laid a cunning trap for the king her father. To punish the treachery of this ambassador and his master, the king applied some invisible mending, as it were, to the small print of the treaty; by rewording it in terms dictated to him by his daughter, he so adroitly turned the tables that it was the deceiver who was deceived. In like fashion, she exposed a vile piece of roguery that a certain minister had a mind to play on the king; and, by the advice she gave her father, matters were arranged so that the traitor's villainy would fall on his own head. On other occasions, too, the princess showed so subtle an intelligence that the people of her country gave her the nickname of Finessa.

The king loved her so much more than her two sisters, and so much more relied on her good sense, that, if she had truly been his only child, he would have set out on his journey without the least unease. Yet he mistrusted the conduct of his elder daughters as implicitly as he trusted that of the younger. And so, to feel absolutely at ease about his family during his absence, and about his subjects too, he took the following steps:

I've no doubt that you, dear Reader, my judge and sometime collaborator, well versed as you are in such tales, have heard about a hundred times of the marvellous power of fairies. The king I speak of, being an intimate of one of these paragons, went to visit his friend and acquainted her with the unease he felt about his daughters.

It isn't, he said, as if the two eldest, who alone worry me, have ever done anything truly contrary to their duty. But they have so little good sense, they're so imprudent, and live so very idly, what I fear is that, in my absence, they will engage in some foolish intrigue or other, merely to amuse themselves. As for Finessa, though I have absolutely no fears on her account, I prefer to treat her exactly as I do her sisters, so that only I will ever know that she's my darling of the three. For which reason, dear fairy, I wish you to make three glass bobbins for my daughters, and make them so skilfully that each of them will break if ever she to whom it belongs does anything to betray her honour.

As she was one of the most expert of the *genus faerium*, she followed these instructions to the letter and at once presented him with three magic bobbins. Yet this precaution was still not enough for the king. He led the princesses off to a tower that stood, high and lonely and uninhabited, in the palace grounds, commanded them to take up residence there during his absence and charged them not to admit into it any person whatsoever, and for whatever the reason given. He gave temporary notice to their retinue of attendants, of both sexes. And, after handing a magic bobbin to each of his daughters, complete with a description of its properties, he kissed them goodbye, locked the doors of the tower, put the keys in his purse and departed.

Now you may be forgiven for supposing, Reader, from what I've just said, that these princesses were in danger of starving to death. Nothing of the kind. Care was taken to fix a pulley to one of the tower's windows: a rope was slipped through it, to which a basket was attached, and that basket lowered at least once a day for provisions. When it was drawn up again, the princesses carefully stowed the rope away in their chamber.

Having never known solitude, Lackadaisy and Loquatia were soon driven to a state of utter despair; and, as the doubly terrible thing about loneliness is that it must be suffered alone, they fretted to such a degree that I can find no adequate words to express it. They forced themselves, nevertheless, to be patient, at least at first, for what the king had told them of their bobbins so terrified them they believed the slightest lapse on their part might cause them to break.

As for Finessa, she wasn't in the least put out. Her weaving, sewing and music-making were sufficient amusement for her;

besides which, by order of the king's regent, documents were put in their basket every day, documents designed to keep them well informed on everything that was happening, both inside the kingdom and out. This was done at the king's own suggestion, and the minister in question, to ingratiate himself with the princesses, carried out his master's orders as if his life were at stake (which it wasn't quite). Finessa would read all the latest news with both attention and pleasure; but as for her sisters, well, they truly couldn't have cared less if they tried. As Loquatia said to Finessa: We're too much out of humour to amuse ourselves with such trifles. Now if only we had such a thing as a pack of cards . . .

Thus they spent their time continually railing against their lot, sleeplessly tossing and turning in bed as if there were a pea under the mattress, except that this pea wasn't under the mattress but right under their skin! How much better, they sighed, to be born happy than to be born the daughter of a king!

They were frequently at the windows of the tower, to see what was happening underneath. And one day, while Finessa was busying herself about some pretty piece of needlework, her sisters, leaning out of the window, saw at the foot of the tower a poor woman clothed in rags and tatters, who cried up to them in a mournful tone, complaining of the wretchedness of her life in a voice that would have drawn tears from a philosopher. She implored them, with clasped hands, to let her enter the castle, telling them that she was but a miserable old woman who nevertheless had a thousand and one skills, all of them practical, and would serve her new mistresses with the utmost fidelity. At first the princesses called to mind their father's warning not to let anyone, anyone at all, into the tower; but Lackadaisy was so weary of always waiting upon herself, and Loquatia just as weary

of having no one but her sisters to talk to, that the desire of the one to have someone to twiddle her thumbs for her when she felt too lazy to twiddle them herself, and the desire of the other to have someone new to listen to all her twaddle, made them resolve to let in the poor stranger.

Do you really suppose, said Loquatia to her sister, that the king's order extends to this unfortunate wretch? I think we can allow her in without any consequence to ourselves.

Fifter, answered Lackadaisy, who had a lisp, you muft do as you pleafe.

Loquatia needed no more encouragement. She immediately lowered the basket, the poor woman climbed into it, and the princesses drew her up with the help of the pulley.

When they had had some time to inspect her more closely, the putrid state of her clothes quite turned their stomachs. They would have given her others at once if she hadn't told them that she would change them the next day: for the moment, she insisted, her only consideration was for the work at hand. And, just as she was uttering these words, Finessa entered the room, startled to see a totally unknown creature in her sisters' company. They told her the reasons which had induced them to pull her up into the tower, and Finessa, realising that what was done was done, could scarcely conceal her vexation at such an imprudent action.

In the meantime, the princesses' new servant took a hundred turns around the castle on the pretence of going about her chores, but in reality to observe how everything was laid out in it. For, my dear Reader (and I can't help thinking you're already a step or two ahead of me in my own narrative), this so-called beggar-woman was as dangerous an intruder in the tower as Count Ory* in the nunnery that he contrived to enter disguised as a fugitive abbess.

To keep you no longer in suspense, I shall tell you that, tattered as she was, aged as she was, she was none other than the son – indeed, the young son! – of a powerful king, whose kingdom chanced to be just next door to that of the princesses' father. This prince was one of the craftiest and most underhand persons of his time and he had the king his father entirely under his sway; which, in truth, wasn't difficult, the latter being so sweet-tempered and easygoing a monarch that his nickname was The Lamb. As for The Lamb's son, what with all his artifice and cunning, he was given the name Rich-in-Craft; or, for short (and no doubt, too, for quite another reason and rhyme), Richcraft.

As it happens, Richcraft had a younger brother with as many

virtues as he himself had flaws. Yet, however different their temperaments, there was between these two princes such a close sibling affection that nobody in the kingdom could understand it. The younger, you see, was possessed of high moral qualities that seemed to find their transparent reflection in the remarkable beauty of his face and the comeliness of his body – beauty and comeliness so very remarkable, indeed, that he generally went by the name of Belavoir, or Beauteous to Behold.

Now it was Richcraft who had put his father's ambassador up to the wording of that perfidious treaty which had been so neatly foiled by Finessa's wit and good sense that it had rebounded on its perpetrators. And ever since that time the prince, who had never had any great love for the princesses' father, held him in the utmost loathing; so that when he heard of the precautions that the king had taken in relation to his daughters, he immediately set out to deceive, if possible, the prudence of so suspicious a father. Accordingly, he got permission from his own indulgent father to leave the kingdom on some invented pretext and took the measures that I've already related to gain entrance to the tower in which, as you've also been informed, the three princesses were confined.

Examining the castle, and observing how easy it was for these princesses to make themselves heard by anyone passing by on the road underneath, Richcraft concluded that it would be best for him to remain in disguise for the time being; because they certainly could, had they a mind to it, call out to such passers-by and have him instantly punished for his rash and tasteless enterprise. He therefore remained all day in his stinking rags and very cleverly pretended to act the part of a poor old beggar-woman. That same night, however, just after they had had their supper, Richcraft suddenly cast off his rags with a flourish to reveal to his astonished dupes that, underneath, he was dressed like a perfect young knight in rich, sumptuous apparel, so dripping with diamonds and pearls you might have supposed he'd been caught in a hailstorm of precious stones.

The poor princesses were much alarmed at this apparition (as who wouldn't be), and recoiled in horror from it. Finessa and Loquatia, who were very nimble both, managed to scurry back to their chambers; but Lackadaisy, who scarcely knew how to put one foot in front of the other, was all too quickly overtaken by the prince.

He at once threw himself at her feet, declaring who he was and persuading her that the reputation of her beauty, and the merest glimpse of her portrait, had induced him to up and leave the pleasures of his own delightful court in order to come and offer her his vows. Lackadaisy was so much at a loss for words she simply didn't know what to say to the prince, who thus had to continue kneeling while she fumbled for an appropriate response. But since, showering her with a thousand tender endearments, he ardently begged her to take him at that very moment for her husband, and since, too, she remembered an old proverb of her kingdom – to wit, that it's no use locking the bedroom door if the thief is already under the bed – she told Richcraft, in a very indolent and nonchalant voice, that she believed him after all to be sincere and would accept his vows. I have to report that these were the only marriage formalities she saw fit to observe – and, to nobody's surprise but her own, she lost her bobbin, which suddenly broke into a hundred pieces.

Meanwhile, Loquatia and Finessa felt profoundly uneasy at what had happened. They had got away separately into their apartments and hurriedly locked themselves in. But, as these apartments were at some distance from one another, and as all three princesses were ignorant of their sisters' fates, they didn't sleep a wink the whole night long.

Next morning the wicked young prince led Lackadaisy down into an apartment on the ground floor at the end of the garden. It was there (whilst secretly dropping artificial tears into her eyes, it being far too much trouble to shed real ones) she told him how very disturbed she was about her sisters and how she dared not see them, for fear they would take her to task for her marriage. The prince assured her he would undertake to make them approve of it; and after a few more consoling words, locked Lackadaisy in, without her noticing that he'd done so, and went off to look for the two other princesses. It took him quite a long time to discover where their chambers were, and he might not have found them at all had Loquatia's unquenchable inclination always to be prattling away to someone or other not got the better of her and caused her to start talking to herself, for want of a second party, and loudly bewail her fate. Happening just to wander that way, the prince heard her and, approaching the door, spied on her through its keyhole.

Richcraft spoke to her through the door, saying to her exactly what he'd said to her sister, which was in essence that it was solely the desire to offer her his heart and his hand that had prompted him to enter the tower in so underhand a style. He praised (by that I mean he grossly flattered) her wit and beauty; and Loquatia, who'd never met anyone before so uncannily echoing her own high opinion of her charms, was foolish enough to believe everything he said. She answered him in a positive torrent of words, and not, I must say, in a manner that would have pleased her father. It was a remarkable exploit in its way, her talking as she did, for she was most terribly faint; having been chattering away to herself from the moment she got up, she had left no room for anything to pass through in the other direction and hadn't tasted a morsel of food all day. Besides, as she was extremely lazy, she was utterly lacking in foresight. Generally, if she wanted for anything, she would trot off to Finessa; who, as industrious and provident as her sisters were the contrary, always had in her chamber a selection of biscuits, pies and macaroons, sweetmeats and savouries, all the product of her own two hands. Loquatia, then, who had no such natural gifts, and was by now almost swooning with hunger, opened her door at last to the young prince, and he, born seducer as he was, wasted no time in pressing home his advantage.

Then they both left her apartment and entered the castle's pantry, where all kinds of refreshments were laid out, for the basket furnished the princesses day after day with more than enough for their needs. Loquatia, to be absolutely fair to her, was still a trifle anxious about her sisters and what might have become of them, and the notion came to her, why I cannot precisely say, that they'd both no doubt locked themselves into Finessa's chamber, where they would certainly want for nothing. Richcraft used every argument he knew to reinforce such a notion in her empty head, and promised to go looking for them that same evening. No, she replied, with the sincerity of the moment, that wasn't quite good enough; rather, they must go just as soon as they had done eating.

In short, the prince and princess heartily fell to their supper; and when they'd eaten their fill, Richcraft expressed a wish to see the very finest apartment in the castle. He gave his hand to the princess to take him there; and, once inside, he started to exaggerate the tender passion he felt for her and the advantages

the young prince wasted no time in pressing home his advantage

that would fall to her if she were to marry him. He told her, too, just as he had told Lackadaisy, that it would be better for her to accept his hand that very moment; because, were she to see her sisters before taking him for her husband, she would find that they would most certainly oppose her. Being, as he un-questionably was, the most powerful prince in the entire region, he would impress them as so far fitter a husband for her elder sister than for her that that sister in particular would never, ever, consent to such a match.

Loquatia, after a great deal of this, and other nonsense just as sophistical, acted as rashly as Lackadaisy had done. She accepted the prince's proposal and never gave a second's thought to the effect it might have on her glass bobbin.

That same evening, however, she returned to her chamber with the prince and the first thing she saw there was her bobbin lying shattered in a hundred fragments. She was so disturbed at the sight of it that the puzzled prince asked her why; and as her fancy for babbling rendered her incapable of keeping mum on any subject, the more so if it were a secret, she foolishly told Richcraft all about the bobbin and what was peculiar to it. The prince positively gloated to hear what she had to say, since it meant that the father of these three princesses could not fail to learn just how much his daughters' conduct left to be desired.

As Loquatia, now, was no longer in a mood to go in search of her sisters, having good reason to fear their disapproval of what she had done, her new husband kindly offered to perform this duty himself and told her that he would find a way of winning them over to her cause. The princess, reassured, and not having closed her eyes all night, grew quite drowsy; and while she was asleep, Richcraft neatly turned the key on her, just as he had on Lackadaisy.

Isn't it true, Reader, that this Richcraft is such a great blackguard you would like to boo the very page on which his name is imprinted? And isn't it equally true, alas, that our two elder princesses, with their feet of human, of too human, clay, are such ninnies, both of them, that you can scarcely contain your anger and irritation at their conduct and are perhaps even now on the point of throwing this book away in disgust? But don't, I pray, not yet. They will all be treated according to their deserts: no one will triumph save the wise and courageous Finessa.

After the perfidious prince had locked Loquatia up, he went from room to room of the castle and, finding all of them open but one, concluded for certain that it was into that one that Finessa had retired. And as he had composed a string of compliments for her, he stood in front of her door and attempted to talk to her through it, deploying all the charm that had so ingratiated him with her sisters. But in this case the door turned out to be a wall. This princess, who was no dupe, no gull, contented herself with listening to him a good long while without saying a word herself.

At last, realising that, despite her silence, Richcraft knew she was inside, she told him: If it's true, young prince, that you have as strong and sincere a passion for me as you would have me believe, then you surely won't mind going down into the garden and closing the door behind you. If you do so, I shall be happy to talk to you just as much as you please out of the window of my apartment.

Richcraft would have none of this. And as the princess obstinately persisted in not opening her door to him (how comforting is a locked door from the inside, how very infuriating from the outside), the prince found himself a hammer and caved it in with a single blow. When he entered at last, however, he found Finessa armed in her turn, with a huge axe which had accidentally been left in a wardrobe near her chamber.

Emotion had fired up Finessa's complexion; but, although it was at him that her eyes sparkled with rage, it was only the sparkle, not the rage, that Richcraft could see, and she appeared all the more enchanting a beauty to him. Indeed, he would have thrown himself at her feet, except that she said to him boldly, as she confronted him: Prince, if you take one step nearer me, I shall raise this axe and slice your head into two neat hemispheres.

What, beautiful princess, said Richcraft, ever the hypocrite, is the love I have for you to be repaid only with hatred of me?

He began to speak to her, if from the far end of the room, of the violent ardour that the reputation of her beauty and wit had inspired in him. He added that his sole motive in adopting so repulsive a disguise was to offer her his hand and heart, and so forth (for I know you've heard this speech before); and he told her that she ought to pardon his boldness in breaking down her door by ascribing it to the passion for her that had prompted so rash and unsociable an act. Finally, he tried to persuade her, as he had so easily persuaded her sisters, that it was in her own interest to marry him as soon as possible.

The cunning princess, pretending to be entirely mollified by his speech, answered that she must first find her sisters, and after that they would decide together what had to be done. To this Richcraft replied that he couldn't allow such a move until she had consented to marry him, arguing that Lackadaisy and Loquatia would certainly not agree to the match on account of their being her elders.

"Prince, if you take one step nearer me, I shall raise this axe and slice your head into two neat hemispheres."

Finessa already had good reason to distrust the young prince and her suspicions of him were only fuelled by his argumentation. She trembled to think what might have happened to her sisters at the hands of such a villain and was resolved at one stroke to avenge them and herself avoid the same misfortune she suspected had befallen them. So she told the prince that she would consent to marry him, but that, as she had heard that marriages made at night were invariably unhappy ones, she wanted him to postpone the ceremony itself until the morning. She assured him, too, that she wouldn't mention a syllable to Lackadaisy and Loquatia of anything that had passed between them and requested him to give her just a little time to herself to say her prayers. Afterwards, she would take him to a chamber in which there was a very soft and comfortable bed, and then return to her own till the following day.

Now, if the truth be told, Richcraft was not the bravest of young princes; and, seeing Finessa still with her axe, with which her fingers toyed as though it were as light and airy as a fan, Richcraft, I say, agreed to obey the princess's wishes in this matter, and went away to give her time to meditate. But he was no sooner out of the room than Finessa ran off to prepare a bed for him in one of the other chambers of the castle.

This chamber was as splendidly appointed as any; except that in the middle of the floor there was a gaping hole leading to the sewer in which were thrown all the kitchen ordures, and worse, of the whole castle. Across this hole Finessa laid a pair of slender wooden poles, then made a very handsome bed on top of them and hurriedly returned to her apartment. A moment later Richcraft came back in, to be conducted by the princess to the room in which she had made up his bed. There he retired for the night.

*

Without even troubling to undress, the prince simply hurled himself on the bed. And as his weight immediately caused the two slender poles to split down the middle, he found himself to his astonishment plummeting to the bottom of the sewer, bruising himself all over on the way down and landing with a loud splash. His room was not too far from Finessa's own, and his descent into the sewer was a noisy one, so she knew at once that her little stratagem had worked. Paragon as she was, she was still only human after all, and it would be impossible to describe the glee she felt at the thought of his discomfort: he fully deserved his punishment, did he not, and the princess was right to rejoice at it. Yet her joy was not so unbounded as to make her forgetful of her sisters. Her first concern, she knew, was to seek them out.

Finding Loquatia posed no problem, since Richcraft, after double-locking her in her chamber, had left the key in the door. Finessa quickly unlocked it and went in to awaken her sister and relate to her just by what means she had contrived to elude the wicked prince, who had come to the castle to insult them all. At this news Loquatia was thunderstruck, as she had swallowed whole every single word that Richcraft had spoken to her and was still convinced of his virtuous intentions. Oh yes, dear Reader, there are such people in the world, even now, and half of them are women.

Attempting to conceal her secret sorrow at this unexpected turn of events, she left her room with Finessa to look for Lackadaisy. But although they looked into all the rooms of the castle, they couldn't find her in any of them. At last it occurred to Finessa that she might be in the apartment in the castle garden, where, indeed, they found her half-dead from both faintness and fright, for she hadn't had a thing to eat all day. Her sisters gave

her what food they had, after which they told one another of
their adventures, Finessa's in particular having a pronounced,
and by no means positive, effect on the others. Then all three
went to rest after having had such a tiring time of it.

Richcraft, in the meantime, spent the most uncomfortable
night of his life, and when the next day finally dawned he was not
much the better for it. He had to grope his way through all kinds
of dismal dungeons, the worst horrors of which he couldn't see
(and it may have been just as well), because they weren't
illuminated by so much as a flicker of light. At last, though, after
a long and painful struggle, he managed to reach the end of the
sewer, which he discovered ran into a river at some distance from
the castle. He made himself heard by some fishermen, good,
ungrudging countryfolk by whom he was drawn out in such a
pickle as to inspire true compassion in them.

Richcraft had himself carried immediately to his father's court
to be hosed down and tended to, but his disgrace made him hate
Finessa so fiercely that he thought less of looking after himself
than of taking revenge on her.

Finessa's thoughts, too, were much troubled. Honour was a
thousand times dearer to her than life itself, and her sisters'
shameful conduct had cast her into such despair that it took all
her will-power to govern it. At the same time, the ill state of
health in which those princesses found themselves, as a direct
consequence of their unworthy marriages, put her constancy
even further to the test.

Since his misadventure, Richcraft, that unrepentant deceiver, had
once again been mustering all his wits to make himself the
complete villain; neither the sewer nor the bruises caused him as

much vexation as the mere fact of being himself deceived. He thought long and hard about the effects of his two marriages so-called; and, to further tempt the princesses, had great tubs full of trees, all laden with ripe, glistening fruit, transported to the castle and placed in a row beneath its windows. Lackadaisy and Loquatia, who would often sit gazing out of those windows, could not but see the fruit and they nagged and nagged at Finessa to go down in the basket and fetch some up. Her good humour was so great, as was her willingness to oblige her poor sisters, whose appetites had taken a curious turn of late, that she did as they asked and bore up the very juiciest of the fruit, which they both immediately devoured.

And the next day there appeared to sprout more fruit and of another kind. This was a new temptation for the princesses, and a new test of their sister's good humour. But, this time, Richcraft's officers, who had been lying in ambush, and had failed in their task the day before, were not found wanting. They seized upon Finessa and carried her off in full view of her sisters, who could do nothing to stop them.

On Richcraft's orders, his guards took Finessa to a large country house where the young prince was recuperating from his recent mishap. Working himself up into a lather, Richcraft cursed her to her face in a hundred brutish ways – a cursing to which she answered with a firmness of character and a greatness of soul that makes me congratulate myself once more on having her as my heroine. At last, after holding her prisoner for some little time, he had her taken to the summit of the highest mountain in the kingdom, and it was there he told her that he was going to put her to death in such a fashion as would finally avenge him for all the injuries he had received at her pale hands. He showed her a barrel all around the inside of which were stuck razors, penknives and nails, and told her that, as her punishment, a punishment she well deserved, he was going to have her put inside it and rolled down from the top of the mountain into the valley far below.

Though Finessa was no Roman, she was to outward appearance just as unafraid of this punishment as was Regulus* at the prospect of a similar ordeal: she retained all of that poise and presence for which, I trust, she has become a byword. Yet Richcraft, who might have come round to admiring such a heroic stance, hated her all the more for it and became all the more resolved to torture her. To that end, he bent down to peer into the barrel to see whether a few more cutting edges might be added to those with which it was already adorned.

Watching Richcraft lean over the barrel, Finessa seemed to see opportunity staring her in the face, and lost not a moment in exploiting it. Without giving her tormentor any time to know where he was, she deftly kicked him inside and started to roll the barrel down the mountain. Whereupon she herself ran away, and the prince's officers, who weren't on the whole evil men, merely soldiers, and who had watched their master torment the pretty young princess with heavy hearts, made not the least attempt to catch her up. Besides, what had happened to Richcraft so alarmed them that their only thought was to try and stop the barrel. It was all, however, in vain: unimpeded, it rolled the whole way down the mountainside, and when the prince was at last extricated from it, his body was bleeding from a thousand cuts.

Whilst Richcraft's accident threw the king his father and his brother Prince Belavoir into the utmost despair, the ordinary people of the kingdom were not at all concerned, Richcraft being loathed by everyone and it long having been a source of amazement that young Belavoir, who was known to have a generous soul, could love so unworthy an elder brother. But so noble was the character of this younger prince that he was deeply attached to all those of his family; and Richcraft had always taken such good care to extend the tenderest signs and expressions of sibling affection to him that Belavoir wouldn't have forgiven himself had he not returned them with interest.

Belavoir, then, was immeasurably grieved at his brother's wounds and tried all he could to have them cured and Richcraft good as new. Yet, for all the attention that was lavished upon him, it seemed that nothing now could save Richcraft. On the contrary, his wounds were aggravated by the day and he lingered on in complete misery.

After so neatly disengaging herself from her plight, Finessa was delighted to return to the castle where she had left her sisters but where before too long she was confronted with that most unpleasant form of truth – bad news. Lackadaisy and Loquatia were each, and almost at the same time, delivered of a son – at which turn of events Finessa was extremely perplexed. Even now, however, her courage would not desert her. Her desire to conceal her sisters' shame made her resolve once more to expose herself to danger, although she knew very well the risk she would have to run. To carry out this new plan, she took every measure that prudence might suggest. She disguised herself in man's clothes, placed the babies of her sisters into two wooden boxes (in which she bored two respective holes where she knew their little mouths would be, so that they could breathe through them), mounted her horse, had these two boxes along with some others carefully strapped to her saddle and, with this queer equipage, rode off into King Lamb's kingdom.

The first thing Finessa heard when she entered its capital was how generously Belavoir had paid for the medicines given his brother, who had summoned to court all the charlatans and mountebanks of Europe. For, at that time, you must understand, there were in our continent a great many adventurers without portfolio, so to speak, without any precise business or talent, who would announce to any prepared to listen that they had received from heaven the gift of curing every imaginable type of illness and injury. These individuals, whose only diploma was in quackery, always found willing subjects among the ordinary folk, over whom they cast a spell with their gaudy clothing and the colourful names they gave themselves. They never stayed in their own birthplace, where people knew them for what they were; and the prestige of having come from a long way off does very frequently, with simple souls, make up for an utter want of merit.

Our ingenious princess, who knew all about such men and their swindles, took for herself a name that nobody in the kingdom had ever heard before, Sanatio. Then she let it be known about town that the Chevalier Sanatio was ready to share all his occult secrets, all his alchemy, with the townsfolk, ready to cure every species of wound, even the most chronic or dangerous.

Belavoir immediately sent for this wonderful Doctor-of-Everything, and Finessa arrived, playing the part to the hilt and some way beyond, confidently tossing out the most obscure medical terms and signing the visitor's book in a wholly indecipherable hand: nothing in short was missing. She was a trifle nonplussed, however, by Belavoir's pleasant, open and honest features; and, after talking to him for a while about the state of Richcraft's health, she told him that she would go and fetch a bottle of her most treasured brew and would in the meantime leave the two boxes she had brought – boxes which, she said, contained some excellent ointments, of a kind particularly suitable for relieving the wounded prince.

So saying, she left . . . and stayed away so long that everybody began to grow quite impatient. Until at last, wondering just what to do next, they heard what sounded like babies crying in Prince Richcraft's chamber. Now this was really rather surprising, as there certainly seemed to be no infants around, but they listened more attentively and eventually discovered that the crying came from inside Sanatio's boxes.

It was of course Finessa's two little nephews. She had fed them before setting out for the palace; but, as they'd been lying there for quite a long while, they wanted to be fed again, as babies do, and were making their wishes known, as babies also do. The courtiers opened the boxes and were discombobulated to find inside them two of the prettiest infants they had ever set eyes on. Their unexplained presence in the palace, however, was enough for Richcraft to suspect a new trick of Finessa's; and, if such a thing were possible, his detestation of her was even greater than before, a detestation that so added to his bodily pains it was feared he was about to die on the spot.

Belavoir, for his part, grieved all the more at Richcraft's precipitous decline; but the latter, perfidious to his dying breath, was reflecting on how he might still abuse his brother's tenderness.

You have always loved me, Prince, he suddenly cried, and I know that you will lament your loss of me. But a man can have no greater proof of another's love than to see him accede to a deathbed request. If, then, I have ever been dear to you, grant me this one request that I am about to ask of you. It's certain I shall never ask another.

Considering the condition in which his brother now found himself, Belavoir naturally could not refuse him, whatever his request might be, and he swore that he would grant him anything he wished.

When Richcraft heard him make this promise, he embraced his brother and said: I die contented, brother, for I die avenged. That which I ask is that you seek the hand of Finessa in marriage, immediately upon my decease. You will, I am sure, obtain it; and the moment she is in your power, I want you to plunge a dagger in her heart.

At these words Belavoir trembled with horror and repented the imprudence of his promise. But it was too late; the thing could not be unsaid. Nor did he want his regret to be noticed by his brother, who expired soon after.

Richcraft's father, a good man if too indulgent, was of course deeply sorrowed by his son's death. But his people, far from regretting it, were on the contrary glad that it secured the succession to the throne of Belavoir, who was as widely loved as his late brother had been loathed.

Finessa, meanwhile, who had once more happily rejoined her sisters, heard soon after of Richcraft's death; and, some time after that, news came to the three princesses that the king their father was at long last on his way home.

On his arrival, he immediately hurried to the tower, where his first concern was to inspect the three glass bobbins. Lackadaisy, who was first to be asked, went off and brought back that which belonged to Finessa; then, making a very deep and modest curtsey, returned it where she had found it. Loquatia did just as Lackadaisy had done; and Finessa, too, naturally brought her own bobbin to show to the king. But some slight insincerity in their manner had aroused his suspicions and he told them he had a mind to see all three together. This time only Finessa dared to show him hers, and the king fell into such a rage against his two eldest daughters that he instantly sent them off to the fairy who had given him the bobbins, commanding her to keep them with her as long as they both lived and punish them as she saw fit.

For this punishment the fairy led them into one of the galleries of her enchanted castle, on whose walls she had painted a mural detailing the history of a great many illustrious women, women who had made themselves famous by their lives of virtue and quiet labour. By the wonderful effects of fairy-art all these figures could actually move, and in fact did so from morning till night; and it was no slight mortification to the two soiled sisters to compare the shining triumphs of heroines such as these with the lamentable situation to which their own unhappy imprudence had reduced them.

To add to their teeth-gnashing chagrin, the fairy never tired of telling them that if they'd been as well employed as those depicted on the mural, they would never have fallen into the unworthy errors that had brought about their ruin; telling them, too, till they felt like screaming, that idleness was the mother of all vices and the source of all misfortune. She further said that, to prevent them from ever transgressing again as they had, she would keep their hands and minds busy for good. And so she did thereafter, employing the princesses in the coarsest and meanest jobs around her castle, sending them out into the garden, in the very worst weathers, to gather peat and pull up weeds, without regard for the softness of their hands or the bloom of their complexions.

Lackadaisy all too soon wasted away at having to lead a life so different from her own inclinations, and died of vexation and fatigue. As for Loquatia, who, one night, found a way of escaping from the fairy's castle, she smashed her skull against a wall and passed away, speechless at last, in the arms of some kindly peasants.

Finessa's great good nature caused her to weep a long while over her sisters' deaths. In the midst of all these troubles, moreover, she was informed that Prince Belavoir had asked for her hand in marriage and that her father had consented to give it, without, I might add, troubling to let her know of his decision; for in those days the desire of the two parties most concerned had the least priority in any marriage plans. Finessa trembled at this news, having reason to fear that Richcraft's hatred for her might have infected the heart of a brother who had been dear to him and she began to suspect that this young prince wished to marry her only to make of her a sacrifice to his brother's memory. Beset by these anxieties, she went to consult the wise fairy, her father's friend, who esteemed her as much as she had despised Lackadaisy and Loquatia.

But she would reveal nothing to Finessa, saying only this to her: Princess, you are a wise and prudent young woman. You would not hitherto have acted so sagaciously if you had not always kept in mind the truth that *mistrust is the mother of safety*. Continue to think earnestly on the significance of that maxim and you cannot fail to be happy, without the assistance of any arts of mine.

Finessa, unable to get anything more out of her, returned to the palace in a state of extreme agitation.

A few days later the princess was married by an ambassador who was dispatched to her father's court in the name of Prince Belavoir, and almost at once she set out for the neighbouring kingdom in a magnificent carriage. It was thus that she entered the capital to meet Belavoir, who had come, on his father's orders, to welcome her to her new home. Everybody was surprised, however, to see how strangely melancholy the prince appeared at the approach of his bride, for whom he'd seemed to show so great a desire; indeed, it was said the king himself had been forced to intervene and insist that he ride out to meet her.

When Belavoir saw Finessa at last, he was as if tongue-tied by so much beauty and charm. He paid her all the required compliments, but in such a higgledy-piggledy fashion that the courtiers of the two courts, who knew how much wit and gallantry he could command if he pleased, believed him to be so very deeply in love he had quite lost his presence of mind. Meanwhile, the whole town erupted in joy, a joy publicly expressed in fireworks and music: and, after a magnificent supper, preparations were made to conduct the young lovers to their chamber.

Finessa, who hadn't forgotten the fairy's maxim, had already thought out a plan. She had befriended one of the chambermaids who had a key to the closet in her apartment and during supper had secretly given her orders to conceal in that closet a bale of straw, a bladder of sheep's blood and the insides of a few of the animals which they had eaten that evening. On some pretence or other, the princess then excused herself, went into the closet and hastily made a puppet out of the straw, into which she stuffed the guts and the bladder full of blood – after which she dressed it up in a woman's nightgown. When she had finished, she returned to the company; and, a little later, she and her spouse were conducted to their wedding chamber. Allowing her as much time as she needed to complete her *toilette*, the ladies of honour then removed all the candles and retired; whereupon Finessa threw the straw image on to the bed and hid herself away in a corner of the room.

The prince entered. He sighed three or four times very loudly and plaintively, then drew his sword and ran it through what he imagined was his bride's body. A moment later, he saw a trickle of blood starting to stain the white bedsheets.

What have I done? he cried. What! After such a cruel conflict in my mind, after weighing it up and down, asking myself back and forth, as to whether I should keep a promise at the expense of a crime, have I taken away the life of a charming princess I was born to love! Yes, born to love! Her charms ravished me the very instant I saw her, and yet I lacked the power to free myself from a promise that a brother, a brother possessed with rage, had so unworthily exacted from me. Ah heavens! Could anyone dream of punishing a woman for having *too much* virtue! Well, brother Richcraft, I have satisfied your unjust vengeance; now, by my own death, I shall avenge Finessa in her turn. Yes, beautiful princess, my sword shall –

In his grief and ecstasy, however, the prince had dropped his sword and had to grope about for it in the darkness: a fortunate accident, for the princess, understanding by his last words that he was about to thrust it through his heart, was determined he should not be guilty of such a folly and cried out from her hiding-place: My good prince, I am not at all dead! The goodness of your disposition made me suspect that you might repent of some promise too quickly made; and by an innocent little stratagem, I have prevented you from committing the very worst of crimes.

She related to Belavoir her foresight concerning their wedding night and how she had acted upon it by substituting the straw-filled scarecrow. The prince, overjoyed to find his bride still alive, admired that prudence of which she was mistress on all occasions and felt infinitely obliged to her for stopping him from performing an act on which he could not now think without horror. Nor did he understand how he could have been so weak not to see the nullity of any promise exacted by artifice.

If, though, Finessa, that paragon, hadn't learned that mistrust is the mother of safety, she would certainly have been killed and her death, too, the cause of Belavoir's own: then generation upon generation would have mulled over, and perhaps thick, arcane histories written about, the legendary strangeness of the prince's feelings towards her. That, mercifully, we have been spared! No, it was prudence, happy prudence, that preserved this princely pair from the most dreadful of misfortunes, as also for the sweetest and most felicitous of unions. For I scarcely need add, dear Reader – if you are still at my shoulder – that from that very moment on they lived, as should all of their kind, happily ever after.

Rhinoceros ran into his palace, where he locked them both up.

✷ *Bearskin*

Translated by Terence Cave

HENRIETTE-JULIE DE MURAT
(Attributed)

Once upon a time there lived a king and queen who had a daughter; of all the children born to them, she was the only one still living. They named her Hawthorn. Her beauty and charms brought them some consolation for the painful loss of so many young princes. Infinite care was taken over her education, with happy results: by the age of twelve she was as learned as her teachers.

As she was both clever and uncommonly beautiful, she was sought after by all the kings and princes who happened to be eligible at the time. The king and queen, who adored her, were afraid of losing her, so they were in no hurry to surrender her to these enthusiastic suitors. Hawthorn, too, was quite happy with her lot, and was afraid of a marriage that would take her away from her dear parents.

Rumours of Hawthorn's beauty spread as far as the court of a certain King of the Ogres, who was called Rhinoceros. As he was a monarch of great power, owning vast lands and riches, he had no doubt that he would be granted the princess's hand the moment he asked for it. He dispatched ambassadors to

Hawthorn's father. They arrived at his court and, on the pretext of renewing a former alliance between the two kingdoms, asked for an audience. At first, people were greatly amused to see such remarkable creatures, and the young princess herself fell into fits of giggles. The king none the less gave the order that they be received with the utmost pomp.

On the day of the audience, the whole court made the effort to turn out in great splendour; but joy soon changed to sadness when it became known that King Rhinoceros was asking for the hand of Princess Hawthorn.

The king, who was listening attentively to the ambassador, was so taken aback by the proposal that he was struck dumb. The ambassador, afraid he might refuse, quickly went on to assure the king that, if he didn't give his daughter away, Rhinoceros would himself come at the head of a hundred million ogres to lay waste the kingdom and eat the whole royal family.

The king, who was thoroughly familiar with the behaviour of ogres, had no doubt that the ambassador's threats would soon be put into effect. He asked for a few days' grace to prepare his daughter to accept the honour Rhinoceros wished to confer on her, and abruptly broke off the audience.

The good father was horribly upset, as he did not dare refuse to hand over his daughter. He withdrew into his study and called for her; the princess flew to his side, and when she learnt the cruel fate that was in store for her, she cried out in anguish, threw herself at her father's feet, and begged him to condemn her to death rather than to such nuptials.

The king, taking her in his arms and mingling his tears with hers, told her about the threat the ambassador had made. I'm afraid, my dearest daughter, he added, that you're going to die; we're all going to die, and you'll have to face the horror of watching us being devoured by cruel King Rhinoceros.

The princess was no less dismayed by this idea than by the frightful prospect of marrying Rhinoceros, so she agreed to be his bride, willingly sacrificing herself to save the king, the queen and the whole country. She even went to tell her mother, who was in a piteous state, that she would go to any lengths for her dear parents' sake, and did everything in her power to reassure her. She watched the preparations for her wedding with a steadfastness that earned universal admiration, and walked to the altar, where the ambassador awaited her, so modestly that everyone cried aloud and sobbed for sheer pity.

She left with the same unwavering firmness. Her only companion was a young woman of whom she was particularly fond, and who was devoted to her; she was called Corianda.

As the kingdom of the ogres was many leagues away, the princess had plenty of time to open her heart to Corianda and let her see the full extent of her grief. Corianda was deeply moved by the princess's misfortunes and offered to share them with her, since she couldn't console her in any other way. She also promised that she would never abandon her. Hawthorn greatly appreciated the girl's delicacy and kindness, and felt her sorrow less keenly now that it was shared.

Corianda hadn't dared tell the princess that she had gone to look for Fairy Medlar, Hawthorn's godmother, and inform her of the terrible fate that awaited the princess, and had found the fairy in high dudgeon that she had not been consulted. She had even told Corianda that she would never have anything more to do with Hawthorn's affairs.

Corianda decided not to add to her mistress's troubles by telling her this story, but it remained in her mind, and she secretly lamented the tragic fate of a princess abandoned in this way by her godmother. Meanwhile, the long weary road could not diminish Hawthorn's beauty. When the ogre saw her, he was utterly amazed, and gave a great cry that shook the island where he lived to its very foundations.

The princess fainted with terror in Corianda's arms, and Rhinoceros, who was in the shape of his animal namesake that day, put her on his back with Corianda and ran into his palace, where he locked them both up.

Then he reverted to his ordinary shape, which was hardly less ghastly than the other, and made great efforts to revive Hawthorn. When she opened her eyes and found herself in the monster's hairy arms, she was unable to stop herself weeping and crying. The ogre, who didn't think anyone could find him disagreeable, asked Corianda what was wrong with the princess, and whether anyone thought he would be pleased by such tantrums. Corianda, terrified by the ogre's anger, replied that it was nothing to worry about: the princess often suffered from the vapours.

Hawthorn had closed her eyes to spare herself the horror of looking at her hideous spouse, and the ogre, who thought she had fainted again, felt some slight movement of human pity. He went out, ordering Corianda to look after her; she assured him that all the princess needed was a little rest.

So the ogre left them alone and went off to catch bears, which was his favourite pastime: he meant to catch two or three for Hawthorn's supper.

As soon as he had gone, the princess burst into tears, threw her arms round Corianda's neck, and begged her friend to save her. Moved by Hawthorn's distress, the poor girl racked her brains for a solution. Her eye fell on a pile of bearskins that the ogre had been saving up to wear in the winter (he was a dreadful miser), and she suggested that the princess should hide in one of them. Hawthorn agreed, once Corianda had assured her that she shouldn't worry about leaving her alone to face the ogre's fury.

So Corianda chose the finest of the skins and set to work to sew the princess into it. But – wonders will never cease! – hardly had the skin touched Hawthorn than it stuck to her of its own accord, and she became, to all appearances, the most beautiful she-bear in the world.

Corianda attributed this unhoped-for turn of events to Fairy Medlar, and said as much to the princess, who happily concurred – for, despite her transformation, she had retained her powers of speech, as well as all her mental faculties.

Her faithful companion opened the doors and let out the pretty bear, who was impatient to be free; Corianda was sure the fairy would guide her, just as she had brought about the transformation.

As soon as her mistress was out of sight, thoughts of her own predicament overwhelmed her; but an hour later, she heard the ogre come in, and pretended to be fast asleep.

Where's that girl Hawthorn? roared Rhinoceros in a voice of thunder. Corianda made a show of waking up. She rubbed her eyes and said she had no idea where the princess had gone. What? said the ogre. Has she gone out? That's impossible: only I have the key. Yes, yes, said Corianda, pretending to believe the ogre had done away with her; it's your fault, you've eaten her, and you'll be severely punished for it. She was the daughter of a famous king, the most beautiful girl in the world, and far too good to marry an ogre: just wait and see what will happen to you.

The ogre was quite taken aback by this accusation and the reproachful cries with which it was accompanied. He swore that he had not eaten the princess and fell into such a rage that Corianda's pretence of grief soon turned into genuine fear, for the ogre threatened to eat her herself if she didn't stop. So she did stop, and pretended to look for the princess; this had the effect of calming Rhinoceros's rage somewhat. Indeed, he went on looking for her, with Corianda at his side, for a whole week; but Medlar had done her job well. She had invisibly guided the pretty bear's steps to the sea-shore, and there the unhappy princess found an abandoned boat. But it's easy to see that, without the fairy's help, Hawthorn would have perished many times over; for no sooner had she climbed in than the boat began to move away from the shore.

Terrified, despite her past misfortunes, by her present danger, and seeing no remedy, she lay down and fell asleep. When she awoke, she found herself by the bank of a fair meadow decked out with brightly coloured flowers: it was a sight to delight the eye. The she-bear, feeling the boat come to a stop, jumped into the meadow and gave thanks to the gods and the fairies for bringing her without mishap to such a beautiful country.

Once she had performed this duty, her first concern was to find something to live on, for she was extremely hungry. She made her way through the meadow and into a magnificent forest, where she found a rock hollowed out to form a cave; next to it there was a pretty spring that flowed down into the meadow, and some huge oak-trees covered in acorns. The bear was not yet accustomed to such food, and scorned it at first; but her hunger became more pressing, and she made herself eat some. She found them very good. Then, having quenched her thirst at the spring, she decided to hide in the cave by day, in order to avoid any unfortunate encounters, and only to come out at night. Another thing helped her to make up her mind: while drinking from the spring, she had seen herself reflected in its crystal surface. Her horrible bear's face had frightened her, and she almost regretted losing her own. However, she was consoled by the thought that she would otherwise have been forced to stay with Rhinoceros, and this enabled her to see her situation and her grisly features in a calmer light. As she was no fool, she realised that ugliness is not such a great misfortune, since beauty may only lead to trouble. The bear continued these moral meditations as she lay in her cave: she found in them a source of true wisdom, and she began to be content with her lot.

Now that country was governed by a young king whose mother was still alive. It would be impossible to imagine anyone so handsome, so charming, so admirable in every way, as this young monarch. He was worshipped by his subjects, respected by his neighbours, and greatly feared by his enemies. He had all the virtues: he was just, clement, magnanimous, restrained in victory, noble in adversity. His people complained only that he seemed indifferent to beautiful women; but he knew that he was vulnerable to love and was fearful of his own susceptibility; the queen mother had taught him that a king must know how to rule over himself before he could rule over others. His outward appearance was as perfect as his soul, and all the women of his court burned with desire for him, and wanted to set him on fire too. His name was Zelindor, and his country was called the Kingdom of Felicity.

If the beautiful she-bear had known the name of that country, she wouldn't have been surprised to feel so contented, for one of the privileges of that blessed land was to be happy there.

Zelindor, being young and dashing, gave a party or went to one every day. He often went hunting, too: he was noble-hearted, and enjoyed war-like pursuits.

The she-bear had already been living there for three months when Zelindor came hunting in the forest. Contrary to her usual habit, she had left her cave during the day to stroll beside the sea.

She was coming slowly back, drinking in the air, which was fragrant with the scent of the flowers that adorned the meadow, when she saw the hunt pass in front of her. She forgot the danger that a bear faces in such circumstances, and stopped to watch.

All the king's companions drew back with terror at the sight of the dreadful beast. The brave young king was the only one who advanced, sword in hand, to run her through. When the bear saw him come near, she prostrated herself at his feet and lowered her head to receive the blow. Zelindor, touched by this behaviour, struck the bear lightly with his sword without doing her any harm; then she rose to her feet and, looking at him with the most pleasing and conciliatory expression she was capable of, kissed and licked his hand. These signs of affection astonished the king even more, and he forbade those of his men who had come near to shoot at her. He removed an exquisite scarf which he wore draped elegantly over his shoulder, and tied it round the bear's neck; she accepted it submissively. Holding one end of the scarf, he led her to his palace. There he had her put in a little garden which adjoined his private study. The pretty bear understood very well everything that was said to her, but when she found that she was no longer able to utter a single word, she could not help weeping. As soon as she was in the garden, the young king came to see her and fed her with his own hands. Her heart, unlike her appearance, had not changed, and it beat faster when she contemplated the king's attractions. What a difference, she said to herself, between this handsome prince and that frightful Rhinoceros! But when her thoughts turned to her own appearance, she immediately added: How horrible I look! What's the use of my finding him so handsome! The bear was in despair, and her tears flowed even more freely now than when she had noticed she was dumb.

Leaving the food the king had given her, she went and lay down on a beautiful lawn that bordered a superb ornamental pond. Zelindor, seeing she looked sad, came and spoke to her in the kindest and most sympathetic way. At this, the poor bear became even more desperate, and fell on her back, as if on the point of death. The king, touched by her state, took some water in his hand, rubbed it on the bear's muzzle, and did his best to revive her. She opened her eyes, which were streaming with tears; taking the king's hands between her two front paws, she shook them respectfully and seemed to thank him.

But you're quite charming, said young Zelindor. I can scarcely believe it, my good little bear: can you really understand me? The bear nodded that yes, she could. Overcome with joy to discover that she was capable of reason, the king kissed her. She modestly turned her face away and took a step back. What! exclaimed Zelindor, won't you let me touch you, you sweet little bear? How amusing! What do you want of me, then? Could it be you don't love me?

When she heard this, the bear prostrated herself on the grass at Zelindor's feet to hide her confusion; then all at once she jumped up again, picked a branch from one of the orange trees that encircled the pond, and presented it to the king.

More enchanted than ever with his she-bear, Zelindor ordered that she was to be looked after with the greatest care, and gave her a delightful rocky grotto surrounded with statues; inside there was a bed of well-tended grass where she could retire at night. He came to see her at every possible moment, and brought her into every conversation: he was crazy about her.

When she was alone, the bear's thoughts were melancholy indeed. The delectable Zelindor had awoken her feelings, but how could he find her attractive in this frightful shape? She neither ate nor slept; she spent her days scratching the prettiest verses imaginable on the trees in the garden. Not only love, but jealousy too had come to torment her. She was sick with misery, except when the king came to see her. Then another anxiety struck her. Perhaps he was married: after all, she was more or less married to Rhinoceros, who seemed even more horrible now that she knew Zelindor's charms.

One moonlit evening, she was sitting beside the pond, which was a favourite place of hers because the young king always liked to walk there. She was recalling all her misfortunes, and crying so much that her tears disturbed the water. A huge carp, which was evidently not asleep, came up to the surface. Don't be so sad, beautiful little bear, said the carp; Fairy Medlar is watching over you and she will make you as happy as you are beautiful. With that, leaping lightly onto the lawn, the carp turned into a handsome lady, tall, majestic, and magnificently dressed. The bear threw herself at her feet. Have courage, my girl, said Fairy Medlar; I have tested your patience for long enough, and you'll soon get your reward. You're not married at all to the ogre Rhinoceros; you're going to wed handsome Zelindor. But keep your secret for a little while yet: you may quit your bearskin every night, but you must put it on again first thing in the morning.

Then the fairy disappeared. As midnight had struck, the princess felt the bearskin fall from her. You can imagine how grateful she was to her bounteous godmother, what pleasure and delight she felt. She spent the night picking flowers, to make garlands and crowns which she hung at the door of her lover's study.

She felt some impatience at the period of waiting which the fairy had imposed on her without telling her when it would end; but she had no wish to prolong it through any fault of her own, cost her what it might, so at daybreak she would put the bearskin on again. She spent her time writing the most charming things. Whether she wrote about her jealousy or about her feelings of love, her heart provided an endless supply of fresh thoughts and expressions that delighted the king: for he read them all.

He had given permission for people to come and see the bear, but she found the crowds tiresome. When one is passionately in love, only solitude is pleasing. She wrote the king a little poem about it, and the lines in which she expressed her feelings were so exquisite and affectionate that he was quite enchanted by them. He had her garden closed; henceforth he was the only one to enter it.

For his part, the young king, as he reflected how clever the bear was, dared not admit to himself that he found her irresistibly attractive. He rejected the very thought, and was determined that his feelings for her should not go beyond kindness and compassion. Meanwhile, however, he had lost his taste for hunting; nothing interested him, nothing pleased him except seeing his bear. He talked to her about everything under the sun, while she, in the sand or on tablets that he gave her, scratched useful mottoes and sage maxims for his guidance.

But you can't really be a bear, he said to her one day. In the name of all the gods, tell me who you are. How much longer are you going to keep it secret? You're in love with me, I don't doubt it, my happiness depends on my believing it, but please, my reputation's at stake: don't make it necessary for me to respond to the love of a bear. Tell me who you really are, I implore you, in the name of love itself, which you know so well.

It was a difficult moment, the bear was hard put to resist him, but the fear of losing her lover made her choose rather to risk his anger. Her only reply was to jump and frisk about, and this made Zelindor sigh bitterly. He went away, and his heart mutinied at the thought that he was capable of such ridiculous feelings.

Zelindor, in despair that he could ever have imagined the bear to be a rational person, made up his mind to tear himself away from this monstrous passion, and, giving instructions that the bear was to be well looked after, he decided to travel. He wanted to leave without seeing her, and so, only taking with him two of his favourites, he mounted his horse and rode away from his palace. But as soon as he set foot in the forest where he had met the bear, he remembered his adventure there; he ordered his companions to go away and leave him alone.

The two young courtiers were extremely attached to him and had been distressed to see his mood so profoundly changed in recent times; they obeyed him, and moved a little way off. The youthful king dismounted, lay down beneath a tree, and began to lament his strange destiny. He fell into a reverie, from which he was awakened by the very tree he was leaning against. It trembled violently and split open; from it there emerged a lady of rare beauty, wearing such a brilliant array of precious stones that the king was dazzled at the sight.

He hastily scrambled to his feet and bowed deeply to the fairy (for he had no doubt that that was what she was). Let time do its work, Zelindor, she said to him. Do you really think that a king whom we deign to protect can ever be unhappy? Return to your palace as fast as you can, and save from despair one whom you have abandoned out of an excess of scruple.

The fairy disappeared after these words. Strengthened by her prediction, which in his heart he wanted to believe, the king hastily mounted his horse and returned at full speed to his apartments.

He went at once to the garden; the bear was nowhere to be seen, so he ran to her grotto to look for her.

The unhappy princess had heard the people who looked after her talking amongst themselves and saying that he had gone away. She had not seen him for three days, and she was completely crushed by this dreadful news. She fell down in a faint on her grassy bed, and it was in that dire state that the king found her. How anxiously he rushed to her side, how distressed he was to see her on the point of death! She was cold as ice, her heart had almost stopped beating. The king cried aloud, soaked her with his tears, and called her by all the most affectionate names.

The sound of his voice penetrated into the depths of her soul, calling it back just as it was about to fly away. She opened her eyes and stretched out her paws to embrace her beloved, believing that she was about to die; but the king's loving words and prayers for forgiveness called her back to life. He begged her to forget his inquisitive questions and swore that he adored her. The poor bear was overjoyed when she heard this confession of love, and they spent the most delightful day together. Although the king was the only one who spoke, the bear never tired of listening to him, and she replied in her own way.

She showed the young king some pages she had written about his absence. He was enchanted by them, and their happy combination of wit and sincerity, sweet reason and passionate emotions, has indeed never been surpassed. Suffice it to say that they resembled the celebrated *Letters of a Peruvian Lady*,* that masterpiece of refined sentiment, which will for ever remain the object of public admiration.

If Zelindor stopped reading from time to time, it was only to throw himself at his mistress's feet and kiss her paws.

Time went imperceptibly by. Lovers have never been able to measure the passage of the hours: endlessly drawn out when they are apart, it flies all too swiftly past in moments of pleasure. The clock struck midnight, and the bearskin fell away, revealing the divine form of Hawthorn. She was wearing a magnificent dress, and her head was crowned only with her own beautiful hair.

It's a miracle! cried the king. Was it really you I tried to run away from? Was it you I was afraid to love?

The princess remained demurely silent, but her modesty only made her the more beautiful. She was also afraid that Fairy Medlar would reproach her for forgetting herself and betraying her secret to her lover. She was still feeling confused and agitated when suddenly the fairy appeared in person.

Happiest of lovers, she cried; from tomorrow, you may enjoy the fruits of your ordeal: you have suffered torments enough. Now, daughter, reward your lover's tender affection by giving him your hand; and you, handsome Zelindor, return to your court and make all the necessary preparations for your wedding with this princess. Once you are united, you need fear no further transformation; but Hawthorn must submit herself to my rule for another twenty-four hours. Go, let her sleep; she needs rest. I shall ensure that, when she appears, she will be worthy of you.

The young king went out, leaving the fairy and the princess together. He was in such a state of ecstasy that, instead of going to bed, he had the whole palace woken up, assembled his council, and said that he wanted to get married the next day; he gave orders to make ready his throne and light up the whole château, especially the gallery. He also instructed all the ladies of the court to put on their finest dresses; then he went to see his mother and invite her to his wedding.

The queen mother, who had just heard that her son had woken everyone up, saw how overexcited he was: he was talking with an animation which had long been lacking in him, and she was afraid that he had had some kind of accident. What he was saying, however, was so reasonable and consistent that – apart from this business of his hasty marriage – she could see nothing seriously wrong with him; she merely asked him who was the person he had chosen. The only thing I can tell you about her, madam, he said, is that you will find her charming.

Zelindor spent the rest of the night furnishing an apartment for his divine princess. This activity was especially delightful to him because it kept her image constantly in his mind, and he succeeded in producing the cleverest effect of amorous elegance.

As the ladies of the palace, aroused from their sleep by the news, had not heard whom the king was to marry, each believed herself to be the lucky one. So they all devoted themselves single-mindedly to the question of what they were to wear: they felt as if they had almost no time to get ready, even though they were not to appear in the gallery until the following evening. More than one had lost her heart to the young king.

When the time came and the palace was superbly illuminated,

the queen and the ladies made their way to the gallery, which shone with so many lights that it would have put the sunniest of days to shame. Young Zelindor, more charming than ever, and dressed in the very finest his tailors could invent to adorn his noble form, at last made his appearance. Letting his eyes wander over the throng of beauties, he said: I confess, dear ladies, that I would genuinely regret not having picked one of you to grace the throne, if she who will soon appear did not justify my choice.

Thereupon, seating himself on the throne, he ordered them to fetch his bear.

People looked at one another, completely at a loss to know why the king wanted it, and whispered: Is he going to marry the bear?

The she-bear arrived, accompanied by two princes of the blood royal, each of whom was holding one end of the scarf the king had tied round her neck. As she approached, the king stepped down from his throne. Gently touching her head with the tip of his sceptre, he said: Reveal yourself, my lovely princess; may your charms undo the wrong I have done these ladies.

Hardly had these words passed his lips when the bearskin fell away and Princess Hawthorn, appearing in her full splendour, eclipsed all those who until that time had had any claim to be beautiful.

Fairy Medlar became visible at the same moment. She herself had dressed the princess, so it is hardly surprising that not one detail was out of place. Zelindor threw himself at Hawthorn's feet; she raised him up with great tenderness and gave him her lovely hand.

The wedding was celebrated with royal grandeur, and the happy couple, enchanted with one another, lived together in such harmony and with such mutual affection that those coarse people who believe marriage to be the tomb of love ought to die of shame at the very thought.

In less than two years, King Zelindor and Queen Hawthorn had two sons as charming as themselves.

While all this was going on, Rhinoceros had continued to look for Hawthorn and torment poor Corianda, whom he accused of having helped the princess to escape. When he returned from his forays, he beat her almost to death, but she was so devoted to her mistress that she would much rather have suffered the worst the ogre's rage could visit on her than learn that the monster had caught Hawthorn.

His searches were thorough, however, and he eventually discovered that the princess was in the Kingdom of Felicity and had married its king. This news made him so furious that he would have devoured Corianda on the spot had he not decided that it would be too pleasant for her to die quickly. He told her that he knew where Hawthorn was, and with the most horribly blasphemous oaths he swore that he would have his revenge. He took Corianda and tied her to the sails of a windmill; he told her that she could go round and round like that until he came back, then he would eat her, together with her mistress, after roasting them over a slow fire.

He was not aware that the good Fairy Medlar was protecting Corianda too. Knowing her devotion to Hawthorn, she put the ogre's eyes under a spell, so that, when he thought he was beating Corianda, he was really only beating a sack of oats, and it was this same sack that he tied to the windmill.

He set out at last in his seven-league boots and soon arrived in the Kingdom of Felicity. When people told him how happy the queen was, he felt as if he would go mad with fury. He restrained himself, however, and found lodgings in one of the suburbs of the capital. He hit upon the idea of disguising himself as a seller of distaffs so he could get into the palace without being recognised by the queen. He strode up and down the streets near the palace, crying at the top of his voice: Gold distaffs! Silver spindles! Come and buy!

The nurses and governesses of the little princes were looking out of the windows, and as they liked the look of his goods, they had the merchant brought up to their room. They were taken aback by his frightful appearance, but they badly wanted those distaffs, and they began to bargain with him.

I'm inquisitive, he said to them, rather than greedy for money. I'm well aware that my distaffs and spindles are worth whole kingdoms; but I'll give you six each if you'll let me spend just one night in the little princes' bedroom. I'm also ambitious, and I shall be highly regarded in my own country if I can claim to have had that honour. Think about it: if you'll pay the price, my distaffs and spindles are yours.

The nurses and governesses, amazed at the hawker's stupidity and tempted by the thought of acquiring his treasures at such a bargain price, could see nothing wrong with the arrangement and granted his request. They told him to come back in the evening, when they would make sure he had a comfortable bed in the little princes' bedroom. He appeared to be delighted. He left his distaffs, came back in the evening, and went to bed as he had asked.

As soon as he was sure the nurses were sound asleep, he stealthily got out of bed, went into the queen's bedroom, which he knew was next to the children's, and from the sheath hanging at the top of her bed took the knife she always carried in her belt and mercilessly cut the throats of the two little princes. Then he

The ogre took the knife, and with it he mercilessly cut the throat of the two little princes;

put the knife quietly back into its sheath and made off as fast as he could.

When the nurses and governesses woke up, they were surprised to find the hawker had gone. They thought he must have said he was in a hurry to return to his own country; he had doubtless left first thing in the morning. So imagine their shock and grief when they went to see the princes in their cradles and found the fair babes bathed in blood, with their throats cut! Their cries were dreadful: the whole palace came running, and the king and queen themselves followed. What a sight for parents to behold! The king's despair, the queen's mortal anguish, the agonised cries of the entire court made that tragic moment yet more horrible. No one could imagine who could be guilty of such a monstrous crime; the governesses and nurses were careful not to disclose their fateful secret. The queen fainted in the arms of her husband and had to be carried out.

All attempts to discover who the criminal was proved fruitless. The king issued proclamations and offered extravagant rewards, but to no avail. Rhinoceros knew the secret, and was quite sure it would not be revealed.

The ogre had gone into hiding in another part of the town. He had removed his hawker's clothes and dressed up as an astrologer instead. He calmly waited until the king's curiosity and grief brought the monarch to his door, and this soon happened. People kept saying in front of the king that there was a wonderful man who could read the past and the future like a book. So many examples were quoted that Zelindor decided to try out this celebrated divine. He went in person and questioned him about the horrible massacre of his children.

The astrologer, who was secretly delighted to be able to wreak still more havoc, gravely told the king that the culprit was to be found in his palace. Zelindor trembled when he heard these words. The impostor went on to assure him that if he called together all the women of the palace and inspected every knife he found hanging in a sheath from their belts, he would without fail discover the murderess, for her knife would still be bloody.

The king, though deeply shaken, followed the monster's advice as soon as he returned to the palace, but he found no sign of what he was looking for. He therefore visited the astrologer again the next day and told him that his investigations had been fruitless. You cannot have made a thorough search, said the unspeakable creature, pretending to be furious that his competence should be called into question. What? replied the king. Did you expect me to search my mother and my wife? Certainly, said the appalling Rhinoceros; I advise you to do so without fail.

Zelindor didn't believe a word of what the astrologer had told him, and returned to the palace very cast down. The queen came to welcome him with open arms. He paled when he saw, as she came closer, a sheath at her side. He took it from her, opened it, and pulled out the knife. It was covered in blood.

Ah, perfidious woman! he cried, and fell fainting into the arms of his attendants. The queen, thoroughly alarmed, asked what was wrong with her husband. They told her.

How terrible! What dreadful lies! cried innocent Hawthorn. How could anyone think I could cut my dear children's throats!

She could say no more, and fell back, half-dead, on to a sofa. The king, opening his eyes, saw her in this sad state; he averted his gaze, and commanded that she be taken to the tower. This was done forthwith, and she was allowed only two women to wait on her. A summary trial was held on the testimony of the incriminating circumstances, and she was condemned to be burnt alive.

Meanwhile, the poor princess awoke from her faint to find herself in that dreadful place. Her women burst into tears, and she asked them whether it was possible that the king could even suspect her of murdering her sons. Not only did he suspect her, they said; she had already been condemned to death.

O heavens! cried the unhappy queen. What have I done to deserve such a punishment? Is it true that Zelindor has accused and condemned me without allowing me to defend myself? I have lost his affection; there is nothing left for me but to die.

As for the king, his heart was pierced through and through. He could not bring himself to let Hawthorn die, guilty as he believed her to be. Seeing that the stake had already been set up, and that the queen was soon to be bound to it, he commanded the palace gates to be opened and went down into the public square just as the innocent queen was coming out of her tower. Her bearing was at once steadfast, firm and modest.

Stop! he cried. His voice was so weak and unsteady that he could scarcely be heard, and the queen continued to mount the pyre.

Rhinoceros, that barbarous monster, had put on a third disguise and taken his place among the people in the square to feast his eyes on the wretched Hawthorn's torments. He urged the people on, telling them, with all kinds of horrible details, how the queen had cut her children's throats.

Suddenly – wonder of wonders! – a dense cloud came out of the eastern sky and burst over the pyre, flooding it in a rain of orange-flower water. Then it opened, and inside, in a ruby chariot, the lovely Fairy Medlar was seen with the young queen's father and mother, the two little princes sitting at their feet on magnificent lace cushions, and the faithful Corianda holding their infant harnesses.

O king, said the fairy, you have been too easily deceived, although your error was excusable. You see now to what risks an excessive affection for your children exposed you. Hawthorn was about to perish, leaving you for ever inconsolable. There is the one who must be punished, she added, touching the frightful Rhinoceros with her golden wand. He's the one who believed he had accomplished his deadly deed, and who maliciously accused the queen.

The uncanny power of the wand held the ogre stock still. The fairy drew Hawthorn into her chariot and told her whole story to the people gathered below. They were enchanted by it; and, as common folk change their opinion with every wind that blows, they didn't wait for the fairy to finish her tale. They seized Rhinoceros and threw him on the faggots, which were already alight. The wicked ogre was soon consumed by the flames.

Zelindor, his eyes streaming with tears, begged the fairy to ask Hawthorn to forgive him. The lovely young queen threw herself into her husband's arms and kissed him tenderly. This touching scene aroused a great cry among the crowd: Long live King Zelindor and Queen Hawthorn!

The royal couple invited the fairy into their palace with Hawthorn's parents. The illustrious company was welcomed there with such shouts of acclamation as have not been heard before or since; the trumpets sounded and the drums thundered for a full week. Hawthorn introduced her husband to her mother and father, who thanked him many times over for loving their daughter so perfectly. The fairy granted them every kind of good fortune, and they lived happily for years and years.

Her suitors would take great pleasure
in watching her toilette.

✱ *The Counterfeit Marquise*

Translated by Ranjit Bolt

CHARLES PERRAULT &
FRANÇOIS-TIMOLÉON DE CHOISY
(Attributed)

Nowadays it is the fashion for women to display their wit in print and I have no wish to be behind the times. Far be it from me, however, to compete with literary giants. We women all have our little mannerisms. Femininity betrays itself beneath the stiffest of styles. However extravagant the feeling or sublime the thought, the attentive reader is sure to detect a certain softness, a characteristic frailty, which we are born with and lapse into repeatedly. Too much is not to be expected of us. A pretty girl, raised among frills and furbelows, should not be asked to write like M. Pellisson.✷ The most she has to offer is youthful fervour, fresh turns of phrase, lively expressions and a fertile fancy. In short, aiming only to amuse herself and her companions with her stories, she leaves exactness, substance and coherence to M. de T., and is content to write better than M. d'A.

Here, then, is my own attempt. Judge for yourselves, ladies (since I address myself to you) but do not read it unless you are over twenty. No – at twenty a girl must look for something more substantial. She should be thinking about being a good house-wife. She is too old for trifles. Moreover, do not begin to doubt what I am going to tell you. I saw it all, heard it all, knew it all; I witnessed these events myself; no circumstance escaped my notice. Certain details may strike you as bizarre. That is precisely why I decided to put them down on paper. I have never thought much of authors who confine themselves to mundane subjects. Well-trodden roads were made for little talents, and if one takes the trouble to write one should choose a subject that stands up on its own, and which engages the reader from the outset, without affectation, eloquence or embellishment. But on with the dance.

The Marquis de Banneville had been married barely six months to a beautiful and highly intelligent young heiress when he was killed in battle at Saint-Denis. His widow was profoundly affected. They had still been very much in love and no domestic quarrels had disturbed their happiness. She did not allow herself an excess of grief. With none of the usual lamentations, she withdrew to one of her country houses to weep at her leisure, without constraint or ostentation. But no sooner had she arrived than it was pointed out to her, on the basis of irrefutable evidence, that she was carrying a child. At first she rejoiced at the prospect of seeing a little replica of the man she had loved so much. She was careful to preserve her husband's precious remains, and took every possible step to keep his memory alive. Her pregnancy was very easy, but as her time drew near she was tormented by a host of anxieties. She pictured a soldier's gruesome death in its full horror. She imagined the same fate for the child she was expecting and, unable to reconcile herself to such a distressing idea, prayed a thousand times to heaven to send her a daughter who, by virtue of her sex, would be spared so cruel a fate. She did more: she made up her mind that, if nature did not answer her wishes, she would correct her. She took all the necessary precautions and made the midwife promise to announce to the world the birth of a girl, even if it was a boy.

Thanks to these measures the business was effected smoothly. Money settles everything. The marquise was absolute mistress in her château and word soon spread that she had given birth to a girl, though the child was actually a boy. It was taken to the curé who, in good faith, christened it Marianne. The wet nurse was also won over. She brought little Marianne up and subsequently became her governess. She was taught everything a girl of noble birth should know: dancing; music; the harpsichord. She grasped everything with such precocity her mother had no choice but to have her taught languages, history, even modern philosophy. There was no danger of so many subjects becoming confused in a mind where everything was arranged with such remarkable orderliness. And what was extraordinary, not to say delightful, was that so fine a mind should be found in the body of an angel. At twelve her figure was already formed. True, she had been a little constricted from infancy with an iron corset, to widen her hips and lift her bosom. But this had been a complete success and (though I shall not describe her until her first journey to Paris) she was already a very beautiful girl. She lived in blissful ignorance, quite unaware that she was not a girl. She was known in the province as *la belle Marianne*. All the minor gentry roundabout came to pay court to her, believing she was a rich heiress. She listened to them all and answered their gallantries with great wit and frankness. My heart, she said to her mother one day, isn't made for provincials. If I receive them kindly it's because I want to please people.

Be careful, my child, said the marquise: you're talking like a coquette.

Ah, maman, she answered, let them come. Let them love me as much as they like. Why should you worry as long as I don't love *them*?

The marquise was delighted to hear this, and gave her complete licence with these young men who, in any case, never strayed beyond the bounds of decorum. She knew the truth and so feared no consequences. *La belle Marianne* would study till noon and spend the rest of the day at her *toilette*.

After devoting the whole morning to my mind, she would say gaily, It's only right to give the afternoon to my eyes, my mouth, all this little body of mine.

Indeed, she did not begin dressing till four. Her suitors would usually have gathered by then, and would take pleasure in watching her toilette. Her chambermaids would do her hair, but she would always add some new embellishment herself. Her blonde hair tumbled over her shoulders in great curls. The fire in her eyes and the freshness of her complexion were quite dazzling, and all this beauty was animated and enhanced by the thousand charming remarks that poured continually from the prettiest mouth in the world. All the young men around her adored her, nor did she miss any opportunity to increase that adoration. She would herself, with exquisite grace, put pendants in her ears – either of pearls, rubies or diamonds – all of which suited her to perfection. She wore beauty spots, preferably so tiny that one could barely see them with the naked eye and, if her complexion had not been so delicate and fine, could not have seen them at all. When putting them on she made a great show of consulting now one suitor, now another, as to which would suit her best. Her mother was overjoyed and kept congratulating herself on her ingenuity. He is twelve years old, she would say to herself under her breath. Soon I should have had to think about sending him to the Military Academy, and in two years he would have followed his poor father. Whereupon, transported with affection, she would go and kiss her darling daughter, and would let her indulge in all the coquetries that she would have condemned in anyone else's child.

This is how matters stood when the Marquise de Banneville was obliged to go to Paris to deal with a lawsuit that one of her neighbours had taken out against her. Naturally she took her daughter with her, and soon realised that a pretty young girl can be useful when it comes to making petitions. The first person she went to see was her old friend the Comtesse d'Alettef,* to ask for her advice and her protection for her daughter. The comtesse was struck by Marianne's beauty and so enjoyed kissing her that she did so several times. She took on herself the task of chaperoning her, and looked after her when her mother was busy with her suit, promising to keep her amused. Marianne could not have fallen into better hands. The comtesse was born to enjoy life. She had managed to separate herself from an inconvenient husband. Not that he lacked qualities (he loved pleasure as much as she did) but since they could not agree in their *choice* of pleasures, they had the good sense not to get in one another's way and each followed their own inclinations. The comtesse, though not young any more, was beautiful. But the desire for lovers had given way to the desire for money, and gambling was now her chief passion. She took Marianne everywhere, and everywhere she was received with delight.

Meanwhile, the Marquise de Banneville slept easily. She was well aware of the comtesse's somewhat dubious reputation, and would never have trusted her with a real daughter. But quite apart from the fact that Marianne had been brought up with a strong sense of virtue, the marquise wanted a little amusement and so left her to her own devices, merely telling her that she was entering a scene very different from that of the provinces; that she would encounter passionate, devoted lovers at every turn; that she must not believe them too readily; that if she felt herself giving way she was to come and tell her everything; and that in future she would look on her as a friend rather than a daughter, and give her such advice as she herself might take.

Marianne, whom people were starting to call the little marquise, promised her mother that she would disclose all her feelings to her and, relying on past experience, believed herself a match for the gallantry of the French court. This was a bold undertaking thirty years ago. Magnificent dresses were made for her; all the newest fashions tried on her. The comtesse, who presided over all this, saw to it that her hair was dressed by Mlle de Canillac. She had only some child's earrings and a few jewels; her mother gave her all hers, which were of poor workmanship, and managed at relatively little expense to have two pairs of diamond pendants made for her ears, and five or six crisping pins for her hair. These were all the ornaments she needed. The comtesse would send her carriage for her immediately after dinner and take her to the theatre, the opera, or the gaming houses. She was universally admired. Wives and daughters never tired of caressing her, and the loveliest of them heard her beauty praised without a hint of jealousy. A certain hidden charm, which they felt but did not understand, attracted them to her and forced them to pay homage where homage was due. Everyone succumbed to her spell and her wit, which was even more irresistible than her beauty, won her more certain and lasting conquests. The first thing that captivated them was the dazzling whiteness of her complexion. The bloom in her cheeks, forever appearing and reappearing, never ceased to amaze them. Her eyes were blue and as lively as one could wish; they flashed from beneath two heavy lids that made their glances more tender and languishing. Her face was oval-shaped and her scarlet lips, which protruded slightly, would break – even when she spoke with the utmost seriousness – into a dozen delightful creases, and into a dozen even more delightful when she laughed. This exterior – so charming in itself – was enhanced by all that a good education can add to an excellent nature. There was a radiance, a modesty in the little marquise's countenance that inspired respect. She had a sense of occasion: she always wore a cap when she went to church, never a beauty spot – avoiding the ostentation cultivated by most women. At Mass, she would say, One prays to God; at balls one dances; and one must do both with total commitment.

She had been leading a most agreeable life for three months when Carnival came round. All the princes and officers had returned from camp, and everywhere entertainments were being held again. Everyone was giving parties and there was a great ball at the Palais Royal. The comtesse, who was too old to show her face on such occasions, decided to go masked and took the little marquise with her. She was dressed as a shepherdess in an extremely simple but becoming costume. Her hair, which hung down to her waist, was tied up in great curls with pink ribbons – no pearls, no diamonds, only a beautiful cap. She had dressed herself, but even so all eyes were fixed on her. That night her beauty was triumphant.

The handsome Prince Sionad* was there, dressed as a woman – a rival to the fair sex who, in the opinion of connoisseurs, took first prize for beauty.

On arriving at the ball the comtesse decided to go and sit behind the lovely Sionad. Chère princesse, she said as she drew near and introduced the little marquise, here is a young shepherdess you should find worth looking at. Marianne approached respectfully and wanted to kiss the hem of the prince's dress (or should I say the princess's) but he lifted her up, embraced her tenderly and cried delightedly: What a lovely girl! What fine features! What a smile! What delicacy! And if I'm not mistaken, she is as clever as she is beautiful.

The little marquise had responded only with a bashful smile when a young prince came up and claimed her for a dance. At first all eyes were fixed on him, owing to his rank. But when people saw her answering his questions without awkwardness or embarrassment; saw what a feel she had for the music; how gracefully she moved; her little jumps in time; her smiles, subtle without being malicious and the fresh glow that vigorous exercise brought to her face, total silence, as at a concert, descended on the hall. The violinists found to their delight that they could hear themselves play, and everyone seemed intent on watching and wondering at her. The dance ended with applause, little of it for the prince, popular though he was.

The acclaim that the little marquise had received at the Palais Royal ball greatly increased the comtesse's affection and concern for her. She could no longer do without her and she offered her rooms in her house, so that she could enjoy her company at her leisure. But on no account would her mother agree to this. The little marquise was almost fourteen and, if the secret of her birth was to be kept, it was vital that no one should be on intimate terms with her except her governess, who got her up and saw her into bed. She was still quite ignorant of her situation and, though she had many admirers, felt nothing for them. She cared for nothing and no one but herself and her

appearance. People spoke to her of nothing else. She drank down this delicious praise in long draughts and thought herself the most beautiful person in the world; the more so since her mirror swore to her every day that the praise was justified.

One day she was at the theatre, in the first tier, when she noticed a beautiful young man in the next box. He wore a scarlet doublet embroidered with gold and silver, but what fascinated her were his dazzling diamond earrings and three or four beauty spots. She watched him intently and found his countenance so sweet and amiable that she could not contain herself, and said to the comtesse: Madame, look at that young man! Isn't he hand-some! Indeed, said the comtesse, but he is too conscious of his looks, and that is not becoming in a man. He might as well dress as a girl.

The performance went on and they said nothing more, but the little marquise often turned her head, no longer able to concentrate on the play, which was *The Feign'd Alcibiades*. Some days later she was at the theatre again in the third tier. The same young man, who drew such attention to himself with his extraordinary adornments, was in the second tier. He watched the little marquise at his leisure, as fascinated by her as she had been by him on the previous occasion, but less restrained. He kept turning his back on the actors, unable to take his eyes off her and she, for her part, responded in a manner less than consistent with the dictates of modesty. She felt in this exchange of looks something she had never experienced before: a certain joy at once subtle and profound, which passes from the eyes to the heart and constitutes the only real happiness in life. At last the play ended and, while they waited for the afterpiece,* the beautiful young man left his box and went to ask the little marquise's name. The porters, who saw her often, were happy to oblige him; they even told him where she lived. He now saw that she was of noble birth and decided, if possible, to make her acquaintance, even if he went no further. He resolved (love being ingenious) to enter her box by accident.

Ah, madame, he cried, I beg your pardon: I thought this was my box. The Marquise de Banneville loved intrigue and made the most of this one. Monsieur, she said to him with great frankness, we are indeed fortunate in your mistake: a man as handsome as you is welcome anywhere.

She hoped in this way to detain him so that she could look at him at her leisure; examine him and his adornments; please her daughter (whose feelings she had already detected) and, in a word, have some harmless amusement. He hesitated before deciding to remain in the box without taking a seat at the front. They asked him a hundred questions, to which he replied very wittily. His manner and tone of voice had an undeniable charm. The little marquise asked him why he wore pendants in his ears. He replied that he always had: his ears had been pierced when he was a child. As for the rest, they must excuse these little embellishments, normally only suitable for the fair sex, on the grounds of youth.

Everything suits you, monsieur, said the little marquise with a blush. You can wear beauty spots and bracelets as far as we're concerned. You wouldn't be the first. These days young men are always doing themselves up like girls.

The conversation never flagged. When the afterpiece was over he conducted the ladies to their coach and had his follow it as far as the marquise's house where, not daring to enter, he sent a page to present his compliments.

During the days that followed they saw him everywhere: in

church; in the park; at the opera and the theatre. He was always unassuming, always respectful. He would bow low to the little marquise, not daring to approach or speak to her. He seemed to have but one object, and wasted no time in attaining it. Finally, after three weeks, the Marquise de Banneville's brother (who was a state councillor) called and suggested that she receive a visitor – his good friend and neighbour, the Marquis de Bercour. He assured her that he was an excellent man and brought him round immediately after lunch. The marquis was the handsomest man in the world; his hair was black and arranged in thick, natural-looking curls. It was cut in line with the ears so that his diamond earrings could be seen. On this particular day he had attached to each of these a pearl. He also wore two or three beauty spots (no more) to emphasise his fine complexion.

Ah, brother, said the marquise, is this the Marquis de Bercour? Yes, madame, replied the marquis, and he cannot live any longer without seeing the loveliest girl in the world.

As he said this he turned towards the little marquise, who was beside herself with joy. They sat and talked, exchanging news, discussing amusements and new books. The little marquise was a versatile conversationalist, and they were soon at ease with one another. The old councillor was the first to leave, the marquis the last, having remained as long as he felt he could.

After this he never missed an opportunity of paying court to the girl he loved, and always made sure that everything was perfect. When the good weather came and they went out walking to Vincennes or in the Bois, they would find a magnificent collation, which seemed to have been brought there by magic, at a place specially chosen in the shade of some trees. One day there would be violins; the next oboes. The marquis had apparently given no instructions, yet it was obvious that he had arranged everything. Nevertheless, it took several days to guess who had given the little marquise a magnificent present. One morning a carrier brought a chest to her house which he said was from the Comtesse Alettef. She opened it eagerly and was delighted to find in it gloves, scents, pomades, perfumed oils, gold boxes, little toilet cases, more than a dozen snuff boxes in different styles, and countless other treasures. The little marquise wanted to thank the comtesse, who had no idea what she was talking about. She found out in the end, but reproached herself more than once for not having guessed at once.

These little attentions advanced the marquis's cause considerably. The little marquise greatly appreciated them. Madame, she said to her mother with admirable honesty, I no longer know where I am. Once I wanted to be beautiful in everyone's eyes; now the only person I want to find me beautiful is the marquis. I used to love balls, plays, receptions, places where there was a lot of noise. Now I'm tired of all that. My only pleasure in life is to be alone and think about the man I love. He's coming soon, I whisper to myself. Perhaps he'll tell me he loves me. Yes, madame, he hasn't said that yet; hasn't spoken those wonderful words: I love you, though his eyes and his actions have told me so a hundred times.

Then, my child, replied the marquise, I'm very sorry for you. You were happy before you saw the marquis. You enjoyed everyone's company; everyone loved you and you loved only yourself, your own person, your beauty. You were wholly consumed with the desire to please, and please you did. Why change such a delightful life? Take my advice, my dear child: let your sole concern be to profit from the advantages nature has given you. Be beautiful: you have experienced that joy; is there any other to touch it? To draw everyone's gaze; to win all hearts;

to delight people wherever one goes; to hear oneself praised continually, and not by flatterers; to be loved by all and love only oneself: that, my child, is the height of happiness, and you can enjoy it for a long time. You are a queen, don't make yourself a slave: you must resist at the outset a passion that is carrying you away in spite of yourself. Now you command, but soon you will obey. Men are fickle: the marquis loves you today – tomorrow he will love someone else.

Stop loving me! said the little marquise. Love someone else! And she burst into tears.

Her mother, who loved her dearly, tried to console her and succeeded by telling her that the marquis was coming. There was a lot at stake and this incipient passion caused her considerable alarm. Where will it lead? she asked herself. To what bizarre conclusion. If the marquis declares himself – if he plucks up courage and asks for certain favours – she will refuse him nothing. But then, she reflected, the little marquise has been well trained; she is sensible; at most she will grant such trifling favours as will leave them in ignorance – an ignorance essential to their happiness.

They were talking like this when someone came to tell them that the marquis had sent them a dozen partridges, and that he was at the door, not daring to enter as he had just returned from hunting.

Send him in! cried the little marquise. We want to see him in his hunting clothes. He entered a moment later, all apologies for powder marks, sun burn and a dishevelled wig. No, no, said the little marquise. I assure you, we like you better dressed informally like this than in all your finery. If that is so, madame, he replied, next time you will see me dressed as a stoker.

He remained standing, as though about to leave. They made

him sit and the marquise, kind soul, told them to sit together while she went to her study to write. The chambermaids knew what was what and withdrew to the dressing-room, leaving the lovers alone together. They were silent for a while. The little marquise, still flustered after her talk with her mother, scarcely dared raise her eyes, and the marquis, even more embarrassed, looked at her and sighed. There was something tender in this silence. The looks they exchanged, the sighs they could not contain, were for them a form of language – a language lovers often use – and their mutual embarrassment seemed to them a sign of love. The little marquise was the first to awake from this reverie.

You're dreaming, marquis, she said. What of? Hunting? Ah, beautiful marquise, said the marquis, how lucky hunters are! They are not in love. What do you mean? she rejoined. Is being in love really so terrible? Madame, he replied, it is the greatest happiness in life. But unrequited love is the greatest misfortune. I am in love and it is not requited. I am in love with the most beautiful girl in the world. Venus herself would not dare put herself before her. I love her and she does not love me. She has no feelings. She sees me, she listens to me, and she remains cruelly silent. She even turns her eyes away from mine. How heartless! How can I doubt my fate?

As he spoke these last words, the marquis knelt down before the little marquise and kissed her hands – nor did she object. Her eyes were lowered and let fall great tears.

Beautiful marquise, he said, you're crying. You're crying and I know the reason for your tears. My love is irksome to you. Ah, marquis, she answered with a heavy sigh, one can cry for joy as well as pain. I've never been so happy. She said no more and, stretching out her arms to her beloved marquis, granted him the favours she would have denied all the kings of the earth. Caresses were all the protestations of love they needed. The marquis found in the little marquise's lips a compliance that her eyes had hidden from him, and this conversation would have lasted longer if the marquise had not emerged from her study. She found them laughing and crying at the same time, and wondered whether such tears had ever needed drying.

The marquis immediately rose to leave, but the marquise said to him pleasantly: Monsieur, won't you stay and dine on the partridges you brought? He needed little persuading. What he desired more than anything else in the world was to be on familiar terms in this house. He stayed, even though he was dressed in hunting clothes, and had the exquisite pleasure of seeing the girl he loved eat. It is one of life's chief delights. To watch at close quarters a pink mouth that, as it opens, reveals gums of coral and teeth of alabaster; that opens and closes with the rapidity that accompanies all the actions of youth; to see a beautiful face animated by an often repeated pleasure, and to be experiencing the same pleasure at the same time – this is a privilege love grants to few.

After that happy day the marquis made sure he dined there every night. It was a regular affair and the little marquise's suitors, who had had no cause to be jealous of one another, took it as settled. She had made her choice and they all admitted that beauty and vanity, however powerful, are no defence against love. The Comte d'****, one of her most ardent admirers, had a keen sense that his passion was being made light of. He was handsome, well built, brave, a soldier: he could not allow the little marquise to give herself to the Marquis de Bercour, whom he considered vastly inferior in every respect to himself. He decided to pick a quarrel with him and so disgrace him, thinking him too effeminate to dare cross swords with him. However, to his great surprise, at the first word he uttered when they met at the Porte des Tuileries, the marquis drew his sword and thrust at him with gusto. After a hard-fought duel they were parted by mutual friends.

This adventure pleased the little marquise. It gave her lover a war-like air, though she trembled for him nevertheless. She saw clearly that her beauty and her preference for him would constantly be exposing him to such encounters, and she said to him one day: Marquis, we must put an end to jealousy once and for all; we must silence gossip. We love one another and always will. We must bind ourselves to one another with ties that only death can break.

Ah, beautiful marquise, he said, what are you thinking of? Does our happiness bore you? Marriage, as a rule, puts an end to pleasure. Let us remain as we are. For my part, I am content with your favours and will never ask you for anything more. But *I* am not content, said the little marquise. I can see clearly that there is something missing in our happiness, and perhaps we will find it when you belong to me entirely, and I to you. It would not be right, replied the marquis, for you to throw in your lot with a younger son who has spent the bulk of his fortune and whom you still know only by appearances, which are often deceptive.

But that's just what I love about it, she interrupted. I'm so happy that I have enough money for us both, and to have the chance of showing you that I love you and you alone.

They had reached this point when the Marquise de Banneville interrupted them. She had been closeted with her agents, and thought she would refresh herself with some lively young company, but she found them in a deeply serious mood. The marquis had been greatly put out by the little marquise's proposal. Ostensibly it was very much to his advantage, but he had secret objections to it, which he considered insurmountable. The little marquise, for her part, was a little annoyed at having taken such a bold step in vain, but she soon recovered, deciding that the marquis had refused out of respect for her – or that he wished to prove the depth of his feelings for her. This thought made her decide to speak to her mother about it, and she did so the following day.

No one was ever more astonished than the Marquise de Banneville when her daughter spoke to her of marriage. She was sixteen and no longer a child. Her eyes had not been opened to her situation, and her mother hoped they never would be. She was careful not to agree to the match, but to reveal the truth would have been a painful solution both for her daughter and the marquis. She resolved to do so only as a last resort. Meanwhile she would prevent, or at least postpone, the marriage. The marquis was in agreement with her on this, but the little marquise – passionate creature that she was – begged, entreated, wept, used every means to persuade her mother. She never doubted her lover, since he did not dare oppose her with the same firmness. Finally she pushed her mother to the point where she said these words to her: My dear child, you leave me no choice: against my better judgement I must reveal to you something that I would have given my life to conceal from you. I loved your poor father and when I lost him so tragically, in dread of your meeting the same fate, I prayed with all my heart for a daughter. I was not so fortunate: I gave birth to a son and I have brought him up as a daughter. His sweetness, his inclinations, his beauty, all assisted my plan. I have a son and the whole world believes I have a daughter. Ah, madame! cried the little marquise, is it possible that I . . . ? Yes, my child, said her mother embracing her, you are a boy. I can see how painful this news must be for you. Habit has given you a different nature. You are used to a life very different from the one you might have led. I wanted you to be happy and would never have revealed the sad truth to you if your obstinacy over the marquis had not forced me to. You see now what you were about to do? How, but for me, you would have exposed yourself to public ridicule?

The little marquise did not answer. Instead she merely wept and in vain her mother said to her: But my child, go on living as you were. Be the beautiful little marquise still – loved, adored by all who see her. Love your beautiful marquis if you like, but do not think of marrying him.

Alas! cried the little marquise through her tears, he has asked for nothing more. He flies into a rage when I mention marriage. Ah! Could it be that he knows my secret? If I thought that, dear mother, I would go and hide myself in the furthest corner of the earth. Could he know it? In floods of tears now, she added: Alas, poor little marquise, what will you do? Will you dare show your face again and act the beauty? But what have you said? What have you done? What name can one give the favours you have granted the marquis? Blush! Blush, unhappy girl! Ah, nature you are blind: why did you not warn me of my duty? Alas! I acted in good faith, but now I see the truth and I must behave quite differently in future. I must not think about the man I love – I must do what is right.

She was uttering these words with determination when it was announced that the marquis was at the door of the antechamber. He entered with a happy air and was amazed to see both mother and daughter with lowered eyes and in tears. The mother did not wait for him to speak but rose and went to her room. He took courage and said: What's the matter, beautiful marquise? If something is distressing you, won't you share it with your friends? What? You won't even look at me! Am I the cause of this weeping? Am I to blame without knowing it?

The little marquise dissolved in tears. No! No! she cried. No! That could never be, and if it were so I would not feel as I do. Nature is wise and there is a reason for everything she does.

The marquis had no idea what all this meant. He was asking for an explanation when the marquise, who had recovered a little, left her room and came to her daughter's aid. Look at her, she said to the marquis. As you see, she is quite beside herself. I am to blame. I tried to stop her but she *would* have her fortune told, and they said she would never marry the man she loved. That has upset her, Monsieur le Marquis, and you know why.

For my part, madame, he replied, I am not at all upset. Let her remain always as she is. I ask only to see her. I shall be more than happy if she will consider me her best friend.

With this the conversation ended. Emotions had been stirred, and would take time to settle. But they settled so completely that after eight days there was no sign of any upheaval. The marquis's presence, his charm, his caresses, obliterated from the little marquise's mind everything her mother had told her. She no longer believed any of it, or rather did not wish to believe. Pleasure triumphed over reflection. She lived as she had done before with her lover and felt her passion increase with such violence that thoughts of a lasting union returned to torment her. Yes, she said to herself, he cannot go back on his word now. He will never desert me. She had resolved to speak of it again, when her mother fell ill. Her illness was so grave that after three days all hope of a cure was abandoned. She made her will and sent for her brother, the councillor, whom she appointed the little marquise's guardian. He was her uncle and her heir, since all the property came from the mother. She confided to him the truth about her daughter's birth, begging him to take it seriously and to let her lead a life of innocent pleasure that would harm no one and which, since it precluded her marrying, would guarantee his children a rich inheritance.

The good councillor was delighted at this news and saw his sister die without shedding a tear. The income of thirty thousand francs that she left the little marquise seemed certain to pass to his children, and he had only to encourage his niece's infatuation for the marquis. He did so with great success, telling her that he would be like a father to her and had no wish to be her guardian except in name.

This sympathetic behaviour consoled the little marquise somewhat – and she was certainly distraught – but the sight of her beloved marquis consoled her even more. She saw that she was absolute mistress of her fate, and her sole aim was to share it with the man she loved. Six months of official mourning passed, after which pleasures of all kinds once again filled her life. She went often to balls, the theatre, the opera, and always in the same company. The marquis never left her side and all her other suitors, seeing that it was a settled affair, had withdrawn. They lived happily and would perhaps have thought of nothing else, if malicious tongues could have left them in peace. Everywhere, people were saying that, while the little marquise was beautiful, since her mother's death she had lost all sense of decorum: she was seen everywhere with the marquis; he was practically living in her house; he dined there every day and never left before midnight. Her best friends found grounds for censure in this: they sent her anonymous letters and warned her uncle, who spoke to her about it. Finally, things went so far that the little marquise went back to her first idea and decided to marry the marquis. She put this to him forcefully; he resisted likewise, only agreeing on condition that the marriage would be a purely public affair, and that they would live together like brother and sister. This, he said, was how they must always love one another. The little marquise readily agreed. She often remembered what her mother had told her. She spoke of it to her uncle, who began by outlining all the pitfalls of marriage and ended by giving his consent. He saw that, by this means, the income of thirty thousand francs was sure to pass to his family. There was no danger of his niece having children by the Marquis de Bercour whereas, if she did not marry him, her notion that she was a girl might change with time and with her beauty, which was sure to fade. So a wedding day was fixed on, bridal clothes made and the ceremony held at the good uncle's house. (As guardian he undertook to give the wedding feast.)

The little marquise had never looked as beautiful as she did that day. She wore a dress of black velours completely covered in gems, pink ribbons in her hair and diamond pendants in her ears. The Comtesse d'Alettef, who would always love her, went with her to the church, where the marquis was waiting. He wore a black velours cloak decked with gold braid, his hair was in curls, his face powdered, there were diamond pendants in his ears and beauty spots on his face. In short, he was adorned in such a way that his best friends could not excuse such vanity. The couple were united for ever and everyone showered them with blessings. The banquet was magnificent, the king's music and the *violons**

he took her hand and placed
it on the most beautiful bosom
in the world.

were there. At last the hour came and relatives and friends put the couple together in a nuptial bed and embraced them, the men laughing, a few good old aunts weeping.

It was then that the little marquise was astonished to find how cold and insensitive her lover was. He stayed at one end of the bed, sighing and weeping. She approached him tentatively. He did not seem to notice her. Finally, no longer able to endure so painful a state of affairs, she said: What have I done to you, marquis? Don't you love me any more? Answer me or I shall die, and it will be your fault.

Alas, madame, said the marquis, didn't I tell you? We were living together happily – you loved me – and now you will hate me. I have deceived you. Come here and see.

So saying he took her hand and placed it on the most beautiful bosom in the world. You see, he said, dissolving in tears, you see I am useless to you: I am a woman like you.

Who could describe here the little marquise's surprise and delight? At this moment she had no doubt that she was a boy and, throwing herself into the arms of her beloved marquis, she gave him the same surprise, the same delight. They soon made their peace, wondered at their fate – a fate that had brought matters on to such a happy conclusion – and exchanged a thousand vows of undying love.

As for me, said the little marquise, I am too used to being a girl, and I want to remain one all my life. How could I bring myself to wear a man's hat?

And I, said the marquis, have used a sword more than once without disgracing myself. I'll tell you about my adventures some day. Let's continue as we are, then. Beautiful marquise, enjoy all the pleasures of your sex, and I shall enjoy all the freedom of mine.

The day after the wedding they received the usual compliments and, eight days later, left for the provinces, where they still live in one of their châteaux. The uncle should visit them there: he would find, to his surprise, that a beautiful child has resulted from their marriage – one to put paid to his hopes of a rich inheritance.

"Alas! My dear Pussy-White, you lone show pity for my misfortunes."

✳ *Starlight*

Translated by Terence Cave

HENRIETTE-JULIE DE MURAT
(Attributed)

O nce upon a time, there lived a king and queen who ruled over a fine kingdom. Their subjects were virtuous and exceptionally valiant – luckily for them, as they were constantly at war with a king who, with some semblance of plausibility, claimed tribute from them. This monarch was called King Warmonger, a name that suited him to perfection. He would arrive each year with his army and ask King Peacemaker to honour certain treaties he'd agreed to long ago in hard times. Peacemaker always refused to give in, partly because the terms of the treaties were draconian, partly because he'd never committed himself to them in the first place.

Peacemaker had a son, handsome, young, clever and valiant: in short, he would have been perfect if he had never known love. But hardly had he left childhood behind when he fell so passionately in love that he lost all interest in his reputation as a warrior prince. Indifferent to the rape of his father's kingdom and the sufferings of its peoples, he had thoughts only for his mistress.

Peacemaker was understandably annoyed by the prince's

behaviour. His capital itself was threatened; his people seemed likely to desert him in despair and recognise King Warmonger in order to save their lives and property, which their legitimate sovereign had failed to defend; and so he decided to have a serious talk with his son.

Izmir (this was the young prince's name) was summoned to the king's levee. My dear son, said the worthy old man, you've seen how bravely my subjects defended your heritage when you weren't old enough to share their perils in battle. They hoped that you would not belie the blood you carry in your veins, and that one day you might surpass the glory of your ancestors. Yet, ever since you've been capable of helping them to avenge the wrongs inflicted on us, you have scorned to take command of my armies. How can this be? The eyes of the whole world are upon you; posterity will hold you responsible for your actions; what will they say of your honour? I have grown old in my labours, I have preserved the glory of this empire; now that I'm weak with age and almost blind, I can no longer help my poor subjects to repel the violent attacks of an aggressor who makes war against us unjustly. I had counted on the strength of your arm: would you betray my hope, dear son? Would you allow me to go to my grave knowing that the crown that is yours by right has been snatched from you? Be worthy of me and of the illustrious blood that flows in your veins. Fly to the defence of those faithful subjects who must soon accept the laws you give them.

Father, the prince calmly replied, it is not because I lack courage that I appear indifferent to the peril that threatens your kingdom. Nor would it be the hope of royal power which would persuade me to take its defence in hand: I see only pain and grief attend the moment when the crown passes to me by legitimate succession. None of these things can move my heart. But you make me unhappy by refusing me permission to marry my beautiful Starlight. That has always been my sole ambition. My mother calls her a vile slave because no one knows who her parents are. My prayers have not been able to move the queen, nor to wash out that odious name, although I begged you not to humiliate Starlight in such a way. Only let me have her, and I'll be a hero.

What! replied the old king with feeling, you would rather have a slave girl than save your country? What of the respect you owe your father? What of the respect you owe yourself? Would you stain your life with dishonour by entering into such a shameful alliance? When the daughters of the mightiest kings wait upon your choice, you choose a slave, a girl with no name, no family, captured in a town terrorised by our armed forces and deserted by its people; a girl saved only because my general is a compassionate man, and taken in by your mother the queen out of pity? You want me, unworthy son, to give you to this wretched creature? You want her to be my daughter? You expect me to cover myself with ignominy and place a slave upon my throne just to satisfy your outrageous desires? Don't take it for granted, and, if you still have any feelings left, cringe with shame at the very thought of such a craven proposition.

Father, said Izmir in a state of some agitation, the slave you speak of so scornfully is nobler in her chains than the most royal of princesses. Her virtue, her courage, the delicacy of her feelings, make her worthy of the loftiest throne in the world. Why should I marry a princess who is intoxicated with her high rank, capricious, and wholly uninterested in me personally? It's true that Starlight has no known family or high connections; but aren't you a mighty enough king to make all this up to her? I don't need any vain titles; love alone can make me happy. Beauty and good character are the bonds that first bound me to Starlight; her virtue has made them immortal, and I'd rather give up all claim to the throne than renounce . . .

Enough, my son, interrupted King Peacemaker; my wishes will be made known to you tomorrow. The prince took leave of his royal father respectfully and withdrew, alarmed at what the consequences of this conversation might be.

The king went straight to the queen and told her in the bitterest tones what had just taken place between his son and himself. The queen, who was naturally arrogant and ill-tempered, easily persuaded her husband to allow her to do as she wished, and assured him that he would soon be avenged. The king was so angry with his son that he gave the queen unlimited power to reduce the prince to obedience, without even inquiring what means she intended to use.

Starlight was the first to feel the queen's fury. She was arrested, and cruel soldiers clapped her in irons. Why do you put these chains on me? she asked them gently and sweetly: her voice was capable of moving the very rocks to pity. If the king or the queen has commanded you to do it, only tell me and I shall obey; but people are mistaken if they think that by treating me so harshly they can force me to give up the delectable Izmir. I can never marry him, but I shall always love him. Without deigning to reply, these barbaric soldiers dragged her violently away and took her to a dungeon in an old tower; it was a place where it was customary to lock up people accused of the most heinous crimes. They threw her into this frightful prison, took care to bolt the doors, and secretly withdrew.

Starlight – beautiful, unhappy Starlight – recognised that this was the queen's work. Such treatment could not shake her spirit, but she was heartbroken that she could no longer see the man for whom she would cheerfully have sacrificed her life. Thinking about him gave her some relief, and she displayed no sign of anger towards her tormentors. She lay on the bare earth, bound hand and foot, and remained in this state until evening. Then an old slave woman brought her some food and untied her without saying a word. Starlight thanked her affectionately, making no complaints of any kind, and the slave went away. A small hard pallet was the only piece of furniture Starlight had to rest that delicate body, all bruised by the irons they had put on her. She threw herself down, weeping hot tears as she remembered her tender lover, and spent the cruellest of nights; but she was suffering for her beloved's sake, and that thought made any hardship seem welcome.

Food was brought at the usual times; she touched none of it. A beautiful cat, as white as snow, came leaping over the rooftops every evening, slipped through the window into that miserable dungeon, and ate Starlight's supper. At night she lay down beside the lovely slave girl and kept her warm: this was no mean service as the weather was terribly cold just then. The hours, which had seemed mere instants when she was with Izmir, now became long years.

Meanwhile, a rumour went round that Starlight was lost. Everyone knew about the prince's love for the charming slave girl and the repugnance the king and queen felt towards her, so it was easy to believe that Starlight had either run away or been killed by the queen. No one dared say anything about it to the prince, and he did not even suspect what had happened: since his conversation with the king, he had avoided his mother, knowing what a violent character she had. He had always seen Starlight in his mother's company: she was so well behaved that she would not have received him anywhere else; but he preferred to forgo the pleasure of seeing her for a few days rather than expose that charming girl to the anger the queen must be feeling towards him. He was also afraid that Starlight might herself use the power she had over his heart to force him to submit to his father's wishes. He would have suffered death gladly to save her from the evil designs of the queen. As it was impossible for him to remain ignorant of the disappearance of his dear Starlight for long, the prince's most intimate friend finally risked announcing to him this unfortunate piece of news.

It would be hard to describe Izmir's grief and despair. He considered countless different strategies, but the only one about which he was quite definite was that he must kill himself. His confidant managed in the end to dissuade him by pointing out that, if Starlight was still alive, as there was reason to believe, the king and queen would condemn the poor innocent thing to death, since they would regard her as the sole cause of the prince's death: he should therefore preserve himself for her sake and wait to see what time would bring. The wretched Izmir accepted this sensible advice, but made up his mind to lock himself away in his private room and only come out if and when they gave him back his beautiful Starlight.

All this came to King Peacemaker's ears just as he received news that King Warmonger, having secured various military advantages and forced all the approaches, was about to appear at the gates of the capital. He went in haste to Izmir's apartments.

To what depths of shame and demented passion, my son, will you sink? said the old man in despair. Like a coward, you abandon your country, your father, your crown. See, Izmir, see the extremity to which I am reduced: feed your eyes on my agony and despair; delight in the pleasure of seeing my old age wither, and with it the illustrious blood of your ancestors. King

Warmonger, at the head of a mighty army, is already at our walls and threatening to scale them. My leaderless troops are on the point of deserting us, and you will soon see a terrible spectacle: I shall be sacrificed to the fury of our enemies. If you are indifferent to your father's interests and safety, if you have made up your mind to let me perish, so be it, I assent; but, in the name of the gods, save your wretched and faithful people; and save yourself, my dear son!

With these words, he stopped; grief stifled his voice, and he fell back on his seat, tearing his white hair.

Izmir, moved to the depths of his soul by this speech and by his father's cruel plight, took the poor old man's hands, held them tenderly in his own, fell on his knees, and cried: Father! I beg you to forgive me. Live, if you want me to live, and grant me also this one last favour: let me have Starlight back once I have defeated your enemies; I'm going this very minute to fight them. Keep your crown, Starlight alone will suffice to make me happy: just tell me that she's still alive.

The old king was delighted to find that his son was worthy of him once more. He embraced him with tears of joy and swore by everything he held sacred that no one had made an attempt on Starlight's life and that he would see her on his return. Persuaded by these pledges and savouring in advance the joy of seeing his beloved Starlight once more, the tender Izmir kissed the king's hands, washing them with his tears. Then a magnificent suit of armour was brought in. It was all shining with gold, rubies and diamonds; his father chose to arm him with his own hands, and gave him a superb mount. Izmir, handsome as daylight, impatient for the fray, respectfully embraced the king once more; then he proudly mounted his horse and went straight to the gates of the town. He had them opened at once and sped out to meet the enemy.

At the imminent prospect of seeing Starlight again, he fell into a delightful daydream which was nearly fatal to him: he altogether forgot that he was in the presence of the enemy, and only regained his senses when he was entirely surrounded and in great danger of losing his life or his liberty.

The advance guard, seeing such a fine-looking knight approaching, thought at first that he was one of King Peacemaker's senior officers, sent by the king perhaps to offer terms; but when they saw that he continued to advance without deigning to reply to their questions, they surrounded him. Izmir then finally awoke from his dream and recognised the peril to which he had so incautiously exposed himself. But, far from being alarmed, he grasped his sword and swooped like an eagle on those who were closest to him: he cut down a dozen in a moment, and forced a passage for himself. Then the others, angry and eager to avenge their companions, attacked him from all sides; but Izmir, fell and terrible to behold, soon made them regret their temerity. Cutting the arms off some, running others through, and sending heads flying through the air, he unseated, killed or put to flight the whole guard. Meanwhile, his troops, who had been left behind by the amazing speed of his horse, had finally arrived. They took advantage of the terror and disarray that the incomparable Izmir had spread among the enemy: bearing bravely down on troops astonished by this abrupt and unexpected attack, they drove all before them. King Warmonger made the greatest efforts to rally his scattering army, but in vain. Izmir caught sight of him, and a terrible combat began between them, in which each showed off his valour and strength with great brilliance. King Warmonger was finally defeated and captured, and his army quit the field entirely.

Thus ended that glorious day. Izmir returned to his camp,

where joy reigned throughout the night, and sent a messenger to King Peacemaker to give him news of his victory. He treated his illustrious prisoner generously, ordering him to be served no differently from himself. At dawn, he gave him a richly caparisoned horse to mount and led him to his father the king.

Peacemaker was beside himself with joy, and ordered celebrations which were to last for several days.

Izmir still thought of nothing but his beloved. He now expected the promised reward, but his father said no word to him about it, and he dared not remind him of it that day. The next morning, however, he went to ask him for Starlight.

How dare you ask such a thing, Izmir? said the king in a tone of absolute authority. You've just covered yourself with glory; how could I give my consent to such craven self-indulgence on your part? Choose a princess worthy of you; speak to me no more of a subject that has already provoked my anger all too often; you would force me to resort to violence.

Thus are promises fulfilled when the fear of danger is past. Resolute as Izmir was by nature, these words struck him like a thunderbolt and he trembled, not for himself, but for Starlight's life. He made no reply; hiding his anger, he left his father and went to find the captive king. He approached him with such overmastering emotion that Warmonger shook with fear.

Have no fear, sire, he said, his voice unsteady and strange, I come to give you back your freedom. It is in my power, I am your conqueror; so accept it from me as a gift. I make one condition, however: as soon as you are back in your own country, quickly gather together your army and come to seize this kingdom, from which all plain dealing and good faith have been banished. I shall myself help you to conquer it.

King Warmonger, astonished by this strange proposition,

looked intently at Izmir, whose face was so changed as to be unrecognisable; he reflected for a moment, then replied: Freedom is so precious, prince, that I would have accepted it with gratitude if you had not combined it with so momentous a gift; but, precious as it is, I cannot accept it. How could I betray my honour by depriving my liberator of a possession which I would protect for him at the expense of my life? I will not stain my reputation in such a way.

O Virtue, how powerful is thy example! Izmir, recalling his own high principles, and touched by this noble and generous refusal, burst into tears; then he told the king about his misfortunes and explained why he was entitled to complain about his father. King Warmonger listened to him attentively, commiserated with him, consoled him, and promised him a refuge in his own kingdom if he should need one.

Izmir, who was still determined to set his prisoner free, came at nightfall to open the door of his prison with his own hands, accompanied him on horseback as far as the city gates, then returned in secret to the palace.

The next morning, when King Peacemaker heard that his enemy had escaped, he had no doubt that his son was responsible. The queen was even angrier than he was. She forced her husband to have Izmir arrested at once, and he was locked up at the bottom of a tower on the edge of the palace gardens; a heavy guard was placed on his prison. He remained unmoved by this treatment, and was only too happy to be alone so that he could think of his love without interruption.

Meanwhile, young Starlight was still a prisoner; but she too cared little for the loss of her freedom except that it prevented her from seeing her lover. When the noise of the public celebrations reached her ears, she guessed that he had been victorious; the old woman who was her gaoler confirmed it, and the news consoled her somewhat for the sufferings her separation from Izmir caused her.

One night she was standing at the dungeon window in the moonlight. It was one of those beautiful moments when the silence of all things in nature seems to give a special power to the imagination, and Starlight's overexcited mind rehearsed all her misfortunes in such bright colours that her eyes, accustomed as they were to weeping, poured out an unstoppable flood of tears, until her cheeks and her breast were quite wet.

Her cat, her sole and faithful companion, had come to sit on the windowsill next to her and was watching Starlight attentively. The unhappy girl did not notice at first, but then the charming cat began to sigh too, and gently wiped away her mistress's tears with her paw. Starlight could not resist stroking her.

Alas! my dear Pussy-White, she said to her, you alone in all the universe show pity for my misfortunes. Even Izmir himself, intent on his glory, has no doubt forgotten me.

I'm trying to solve your problems, lovely Starlight, replied the cat; and to begin with, let me tell you that your lover isn't in the least ungrateful. He's been locked up in a tower by his father and he's suffering just as much as you are.

Many people will doubtless be surprised that Starlight didn't faint when she heard a cat talking. But quite apart from the fact that the animal was saying extremely interesting things (she was after all speaking of Izmir), Starlight had greatly improved her mind by reading fairy tales: indeed, all the intelligentsia of that country spent their time studying nothing else. To be quite honest, she *was* somewhat taken aback; but, far from being frightened, she took the cat in her arms and sat down on her little pallet to listen more comfortably to what else she might have to say.

What! my little Pussy-White, said Starlight, covering the pretty animal with kisses, you take an interest in my sufferings? But yes, sweet Starlight, replied the cat, and you'll soon see how.

Then she jumped to the ground, and suddenly turned into a tall beautiful woman, dressed in ermine, with strings of diamonds in scallops on her skirt and a stunning coiffure.

When Starlight saw this sudden transformation, she threw herself at the fairy's feet. Rise, lovely Starlight, said the fairy, kissing her; I am Ermine-White, and I generally live in this tower so that I can help the wretches who are imprisoned here, sometimes as unjustly as you are. But I presided at your birth, and you are the daughter of the great and powerful King of Arabia the Blest, so I have a special reason for caring for you. I cannot turn aside the destiny that pursues you; but I wanted at least to console you, because you have a kind heart, as I see from the care you took of me in the form I temporarily assumed. I judged you worthy of my help and of my favours, and you are about to see what they can do.

Starlight was so carried away by all this, and so ecstatic to hear that her family was as good as her lover's, that it never once occurred to her to interrupt Fairy Ermine-White. But as she had said that Izmir was in prison, she ventured to ask her why, and whether she would not deign to protect him also. The fairy satisfied her curiosity about the prince's imprisonment, adding that she could do nothing for him just yet.

But, dear child, she went on, I am this very moment going to provide you with the means to see him and console him. Meanwhile, take this little box, and remember not to open it except in the hour of your greatest peril. I shall always protect you if you do not reveal this secret to your lover. I shall now arrange your exit from the tower: that is all I can do for you at present.

With these words, the fairy tapped the dungeon walls with her wand. The stones gently collapsed, then rearranged themselves at once, in the cleverest way imaginable, to form a broad, spacious stairway. The fairy kissed Starlight again and made her promise that she would never tell her lover who had set her free; then Starlight tripped ecstatically down this wonderful stairway and found herself on an immense plain that stretched out on one side of her tower. When she turned round, she saw with astonishment that the stones that had formed the stairway had risen of their own accord and resumed their original position, as if the job had been done by skilled workmen. Then she left the spot and made her way directly to the tower where the prince was imprisoned. It was in a corner of the palace grounds and was entirely surrounded by guards, except on the side where the plain was, for on that side there was only a single narrow window with stout bars; a sentry was on watch day and night on the flat roof of the tower.

Starlight trembled as she drew near Izmir's prison. Thick clouds concealed her approach, and she reached the little window without being seen. Then the moon came out, giving her enough light to make out her beloved Izmir. He was lying on a reed mattress, pale, disfigured, almost motionless. But one cannot deceive the eyes of a woman in love.

Izmir! dearest Izmir! she softly cried; your Starlight is here: love has brought her back to you. Come close, dear prince, come and reassure her that you still love her. I only wish I were able to reach you! The sound of this beloved voice went straight to

Izmir's heart and aroused all his senses. He staggered to his feet and managed to summon up enough strength to reach the window, where Starlight, charming as ever, stood holding out her arms to him.

Queen of my life, delight of my soul! cried the amorous prince, kissing Starlight's hands a thousand times; is it really you? He lacked the strength to say more. He was so overcome by joy and pain that he thought he would faint; if the beautiful princess had not been holding him, he would have fallen to the ground. Tears poured from his eyes – Starlight's hands were wet with them – and this gave him some relief.

His beloved was scarcely in a better state, but at last, after a long silence more eloquent than the most graceful of speeches, they began to talk about their shared misfortunes. They asked each other a hundred questions, said the same things a thousand times, and exchanged vows of eternal passion.

Starlight did not yet tell her lover how she had escaped from the tower where the queen had imprisoned her, but she had the pleasure of informing him that she was a princess by birth. As Izmir felt that this went without saying, he was not in the least surprised, and did not even ask how she knew.

He spoke only of the quickest way of being with her again. He had no doubt that the king would set him free as soon as he heard that Starlight had escaped, so he advised her to leave this dangerous place at once. He begged her to hide her beauty as best she could, swearing that he would die without fail if he should ever hear that another man loved her and was fortunate enough to gain her favour.

My heart is yours for ever, dear prince, Starlight tenderly replied; never doubt my constancy: I would rather die than be unfaithful to you.

Reassured by this, the prince implored Starlight to let him know as soon as she could where she had chosen to seek refuge: she could send the letter, he said, to his confidant Myrtiz, a young lord who was entirely devoted to him. He pointed out to her the village at the other end of the plain, saying that it was a place where she could wait for him for a few days. They were thus busy making their arrangements when a great white cat flashed past, crying: Run, girl, run: the king's men are coming, and they mean to kill you. Fear possessed the lovers. Taken by surprise, Starlight could see no other way of avoiding the posse than to wrap herself up in her cloak and hide in a particularly thick bush which had sprung up at the foot of the tower.

Just in time: for Peacemaker had in fact been informed that Starlight was no longer in the dungeon and had at once ordered guardsmen and musketeers to mount their horses and hunt her down. It was his intention to have her burnt alive; but, although the troops passed close to where Starlight was hiding, they failed to see her and ran off in all directions. As soon as they had gone, the poor princess, trembling with fear, came up to the window, where Izmir stood almost dead with fright for her sake. Starlight cut a lock of her beautiful fair hair and gave it to the prince as a pledge of her love. Then fear lent her wings, and she ran towards the hamlet with such lightness that the grass scarcely bent beneath her feet; they were bare, and her legs, like ivory columns, dimmed the whiteness of the lilies and daisies.

But the princess was so agitated that she lost her way. When dawn came, finding herself on the edge of a vast forest, she ventured in. After walking for an hour, she came to a fine lawn watered by a rustic spring in the shade of oaks as old as time and prodigiously high. Overcome with fatigue, Starlight chose this spot to sit and rest.

Then, recalling all her misfortunes and comparing the brief moment of happiness she had spent with her lover to the immense passage of time she might have to endure before she met him again, she shed so many tears that the ground was wet with them. The sweetness of sleep had become unfamiliar to her; but now she grew drowsy, her eyes closed, and she fell into a deep sleep.

Now this forest had for many centuries been the home of the yellow centaurs. It was the refuge they had chosen after that unfortunate business with the Lapiths at the wedding of Pirithous.* A number of them who were out hunting happened to pass close by the place where Starlight was sleeping. They were so struck by the novelty of the sight, and by her ravishing beauty, that they stopped, and they were soon joined by many others. Opening her eyes, the princess was extremely alarmed to find herself alone in a wood amid a crowd of such creatures; but when she saw the centaurs looking at her with wonder, and saying to one another that she must surely be a fairy or some kind of divinity, her fear soon faded away.

Men have schemed to destroy me, she said to herself, and the only man I might turn to is not in a position to help me; so why not put these creatures to the test? They are perhaps less barbarous. Besides, I have little hope of escaping: I can only appeal to them to protect me. After these brief reflections, the princess lifted her eyes modestly and addressed the centaurs.

My friends, she said, you see before you an unhappy girl who is trying to escape the anger of a powerful king. Grant me refuge in your midst. All I can offer you in return is gratitude, and my friendship, if you will accept it.

The centaurs were not especially given to paying compliments, but they were open and sincere; they replied that they would be delighted if she would stay with them, and that they would protect her with pleasure.

Then one of them told her to climb on its back, the others helped her, and the whole group set off. They took Starlight to a vast cavern where a number of centauresses lived: she was placed in their care.

The centauresses received Starlight with great joy and did everything to make her comfortable. Every day they arranged different entertainments for her, such as hunting, fishing, and jousting between the strongest of the centaurs. Starlight gave out the prizes – a flower, a crown of oak-leaves – and they received them from her hand with more satisfaction than if they had won an empire.

As they loved and respected her, they were genuinely sorry to see her always so sad and lonely, and one day, they asked her to tell them the reason for her sorrow. Starlight trusted them and couldn't refuse. When they heard her story, they were deeply touched, and the princess, taking advantage of their sympathy, added: Since you are so well disposed towards me, one of you must go to the court and invite Izmir to come *to hunt a white doe with silver feet* who has taken refuge in this forest; he will immediately understand what is meant. She was unable to continue, and shed torrents of tears. The centaurs were coarse, but they were good-natured and warm-hearted; they swore not only to carry out her errand, but also to devastate her persecutor's kingdom, and even put him to death if she wanted.

God forbid, cried the princess, that I should use your friendship to take my revenge in such a way. Izmir's father will always be respected by Starlight, and I would give my life to defend his.

The centaurs' feelings were by nature simple and upright, and this generous sentiment gave them new cause to respect Starlight. One of them was chosen to go to King Peacemaker's court; as his mind was sharp and he was full of good sense, Starlight had reason to hope that his mission would succeed.

Meanwhile, with the help of the centaurs, she built for herself a little cabin to which she often withdrew to give vent to her tears for her lover's sake. The forest was so dense and so full of centaurs that no one dared come near. According to an old tradition which was repeated throughout the whole country, they ate men: this universal terror ensured the particular safety of the princess. She lived there in the deepest tranquillity, disturbed only by the pangs of an unquiet love.

The centaur chosen as an envoy soon reached the capital city. He heard that, when Izmir was released from the tower, he had at

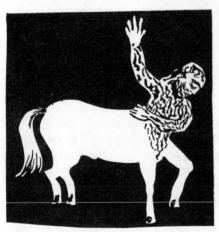

once fallen into a mood so black that the doctors despaired of curing him. The king, it seemed, deeply anxious about the state of his kingdom, invented fresh entertainments every day to dispel his son's melancholy; but the prince took no part in them, refused to see anyone, and shut himself away most of the time.

The centaur had no difficulty in diagnosing Izmir's illness. As he wanted to avoid betraying his secret, he decided to present himself boldly in the king's gardens, hoping that this would attract Izmir's curiosity. The sight of such an extraordinary creature caused a great stir at court, and considerable alarm. The centaur walked gravely up and down, bowing to those who dared to look out of the windows. At first, people talked of killing him; but, apart from the fact that this would not have been easy, they were afraid that the other centaurs would come and avenge his death, so the project was abandoned.

He appeared every day at the same times, fed on fruit, and slept on a well-kept lawn at the far end of the palace gardens.

Eventually, certain court personages who were braver than the others took the risk of approaching him, and even shared his walks. This show of audacity was regarded as sublimely courageous: ever since the centaur had taken the garden over, no one had been seen there. People now began to come closer. They offered him milk and fruit; he ate and drank, and gracefully expressed his thanks. This easy familiarity was considered most charming. Everyone came running to join in, and the company became so numerous that the centaur occasionally found that it was a little too much for him. They talked to him and asked him all kinds of questions: as his answers were rather ambiguous, it was soon being said that he was amazingly clever. Those who understood him least praised him most; some fools learnt his sayings by heart, and bigger fools wrote them down. That is the origin of all those books that people only pretend to understand,

and of the form of speech that was later called persiflage, a word no academy has so far been able to define.

These absurdities amused the centaur for a while, but he soon grew weary of being so much in fashion, and of not seeing Izmir. His reputation became firmly established, as has happened to many people, by the very thing that should have made him lose it. He was the only one to be astonished by this phenomenon: he had not yet learnt that there are times of madness when the fools set the tone, just as there are ages when reason and good sense prevail because the fools are taking a rest or have fallen into their second childhood.

The marvellous centaur was talked about so much, and his sayings were so often repeated, that even Izmir in his solitude came to hear of it. He paid little attention at first, but he was so exasperated by the few people whom he permitted to see him that he went down one morning into the gardens. The crowd that surrounded the centaur fell back a little out of respect, and people cried out: Give way, give way to the prince. Even without these cries, the centaur would have recognised Izmir, for Starlight had painted him to the life. The prince found the yellow centaur a wonderful specimen of his kind; the centaur marvelled no less at Izmir's graceful and majestic bearing.

Sire, he said with a bow, I have long wished to count myself as one of your friends, and I have come to ask you to grant me a favour. The prince gestured to the crowd to move still further away, and replied in the friendliest terms. The centaur, not wishing to make Starlight's secret too public, suggested that Izmir should come to their forest to hunt the doe with silver feet.

The prince, inspired by the illuminating power of love, immediately solved the riddle. He was astonished that Starlight had not been devoured by the centaurs, among whom, as he realised, she had taken refuge. He gazed deep into the centaur's eyes, in order to see to the very bottom of his soul; finding him calm and unruffled, he promised to set out the next morning at daybreak to hunt in the yellow forest, if the centaur would show him the way.

That is my plan, sire, replied the centaur; but come alone, and allow my compatriots to guarantee your safety. You'll find that you have no better friends in the world.

Izmir gave the centaur countless assurances of good will, and spent the rest of the day with him inquiring about the manners, laws and customs of the centaur race. Charmed by their emissary, he was reluctant to leave his side; he took his supper with him and lay down to sleep next to him on the lawn. The centaur was delighted with this show of trust, and, seeing that they were alone, at last revealed to Izmir the whole secret of his embassy. The name of Starlight was often on his lips; Izmir felt as if he would die of joy, and hardly knew how to express his gratitude. He was unable to sleep that night: dawn, it seemed to him, was too slow in coming. At the first glimmer of daylight he woke the good centaur, who – as he was not in love – was still fast asleep.

The prince had himself and the centaur magnificently armed; then he mounted him and they made off with all speed. As they went, Izmir promised that as soon as his father had pardoned him for marrying Starlight, he would send an embassy to seal a lasting peace with the centaur republic, and would choose a thousand of them for his personal guard. The conversation frequently reverted to the princess, and when the yellow forest came within sight, Izmir was racked with violent emotions. They thrust their way with extreme difficulty into the thick of the woods. The prince would take not a moment's rest, and they came at last to

Starlight's little cabin; she was there. As soon as the tender lovers caught sight of one another, they ran into each other's arms, fell into a close embrace, and surrendered to the pleasure of being together again. Their tenderness so captivated the centaurs and centauresses that their eyes filled with tears. Starlight noticed that Izmir had been injured by the sharp thorns with which the entrance to the forest bristled. She made him lie down on a bed of grass in her little hut, fed him, and, with her delicate white hands, applied to his wounds certain herbs whose healing power she had learnt from the centauresses. She would never allow anyone to share these tender ministrations with her. Soon Izmir was cured: love often cures those who are more gravely ill. The prince was perfectly happy to stay with his mistress among the good centaurs; but Starlight would only receive his faith, and give him hers, with the consent of those to whom she owed her existence. Except for that, their happiness was unmarred.

Izmir saw that the princess was determined to carry out her plan. He suggested that they should put to sea, and Starlight agreed, convinced that the fairy would guide them. They announced their departure. The centaurs were genuinely distressed to see them go, but they accompanied Izmir and Starlight as far as the seashore. The young people left behind them in that wild place a memory of their charm and virtue which tradition still preserves.

They did not need to wait long on the shore, for they soon noticed the prettiest ship in the world standing at anchor. When they came closer, they were astonished to see that it was made of cedar and rosewood; the rigging consisted of garlands of flowers, and the sails were of gold muslin embroidered all over with great cats. A hundred white angoras were the sailors. Starlight had no difficulty in guessing that this marvellous ship was another sign of Fairy Ermine-White's bounty. She invited the young prince to embark, and they set foot on board together to the accompaniment of much mewing from the cats, who set up a tremendous racket to celebrate the couple's arrival.

The young lovers had no reason to regret their trust in the fairy. The ship was well stocked not only with all the necessities, but also with splendid and elegant clothes in every possible colour and for every season. The ship put to sea and was driven along by a favourable wind. The white cats were wonderful sailors, and when the weather was calm, they gave superb concerts on fine instruments; the princess, to amuse herself, got them to teach her to play the guitar.

Izmir was delighted to be able to see the princess at all hours of the day without others being present and told her endlessly of his love. Every time he spoke, she felt she was hearing him for the first time, and she replied with pledges of eternal affection. They were apart only at night, and were as impatient to see one another again the next day as if they had suffered the hardship of a long absence.

It was difficult to keep a secret amid all these expressions of love. Izmir noticed that Starlight always suppressed certain details when she told the story of her imprisonment. He complained so tenderly and pressed her so hard that Starlight could not help confessing that Fairy Ermine-White had revealed the secret of her birth, and she finally told him what the fairy had so insisted she should keep hidden. She congratulated herself for letting her lover into the secret, but she soon suffered for it: the sea rose up in fury, thick clouds covered the sky, lightning flashed horribly and frightful clashes of thunder rent the air.

Starlight saw only too clearly that the fairy was taking her revenge. She implored her to relent and punish no one but her,

When it became absolutely impossible
to avoid engaging in combat, only the ladies
fought, throwing crab apples from a distance.

since she alone was guilty. She scorned to make use of the box that Ermine-White had given her: although it would have saved her own life, it might perhaps not have saved her lover's. Instead, she ran to him and threw herself into his arms so that she would at least have the pleasure of expiring with him. Izmir urged her in vain to open the box. Since it can only save me, she replied, I regard it as useless. Hardly had she said these words when the thunder fell on the ship with a terrible crash and cast it down into the depths of the sea. The two lovers rose to the surface, clasped tightly together, and were swept away by the current. A wave separated them; the darkness of the night and the wildness of the sea prevented them from finding one another again, and they were carried separately into different countries.

Izmir had fainted with grief. He floated on the surface until he was seen by some fishermen, who jumped into the sea and took him home with them.

The country where he was cast up was called Quietlife Island. Not a sound was to be heard there; everyone spoke in whispers and walked on tiptoe. There were no quarrels, and hardly any wars. When it became absolutely impossible to avoid engaging in combat, only the ladies fought, throwing crab-apples from a distance. The men kept well away: they slept until midday, plied their spinning wheels, tied pretty bows, took the children for walks, and made their faces up with rouge and beauty spots. They nursed Izmir with such gentle care that he soon recovered and opened his eyes. When he saw these men all round him, but no sign of Starlight, he yelled so loudly that he frightened the fishermen. They stopped their ears and signalled to him to keep his voice down. So he told them in whispers the reason for his despair, and the good people cried their eyes out. Just then, however, their wives, who had been out hunting, came home and told them to go away. Izmir explained why their husbands had been so upset, and they offered him their sympathy with marked firmness, even with a touch of severity. Izmir spent the night in the hut. The next day, as a mark of gratitude for the hospitality he had been shown, he gave these masterful women heaps of jewels; they took no interest in them and passed them on to their husbands.

The prince left; crossing a vast plain, he reached a town built entirely of rock crystal and shining like the sun. He went in, hoping to find his darling Starlight there, and made his way through many streets; he met hardly a soul. Eventually, he came to a superb palace made of the most beautiful crystal ever seen and entered the courtyard to take a rest. He sat there on a bench gazing at this magnificent building; then he walked round it several times, but was astonished to find no door.

The people of the country didn't care for doors because they made too much noise. When someone visited them, they would let down silk ladders, and the visitor would enter through the windows, leaving by the same route. They had no staircases either: it would have been too easy to come and see them. They regarded all visits as tiresome, tedious and superfluous.

This palace was the king's residence. His ministers, absorbed in the important task of teaching the baby princesses to walk, caught sight of Izmir. He was magnificently dressed, and they imagined that he must be some foreign ambassador. They immediately put the princesses back in their cradles and, letting down a huge blue velvet bag suspended on silk cords, signalled to the prince to get in. Izmir understood, and was at once hauled up into a luxuriously furnished apartment.

There he saw, as he came closer, a canopied bed; the bed-curtains were of some rich fabric, and were hung on purple and gold cords. Twenty phials in which the choicest of perfumes were burning surrounded the bed; the monarch, lying at his ease, was listening attentively as his chancellor read him the story of Bluebeard.

Izmir was astonished to see this man with a wonderfully rounded figure, a bright pink complexion and a crown on his head, and he could not doubt that this was the king.

Sire, he said, with a chivalrous bow, I trust you are not ill? No, my child, he replied in a low voice, I'm in the best of health. I'm just having a little rest while the queen is out at the wars.

Shame on you, Izmir replied sharply; how can you do such a thing? You let your wife go and fight in the wars while you take your ease? It's quite unforgivable. My son, the king replied, those have been our laws and customs since time immemorial. If you wish, my chancellor will read them to you; as for me, I've never felt inclined to make the effort to learn them.

This spectacle of cowardice threw Izmir into a noble fury. He seized a stout lance, which was the only one that existed in the whole empire and was in any case never used, and with it he gave the effeminate king a thorough beating. Then he pulled the bedcovers off with some violence and threw them out of the window.

He was about to do the same thing to the chancellor and ministers, but they began to cry in unison with their beloved master and begged Izmir to calm down. As he was naturally kind-hearted, he soon relented; but he said to the king: Sire, if you don't promise to abolish your absurd customs and go to war like other kings, I shall knock down your fine crystal palace. I shall be glad to go with you, but it must be right away, otherwise

I shall beat the living daylights out of you, your chancellor, and those vermin you call ministers.

I leave to your imagination the fright he gave them. The poor king, crying his eyes out, swore to do anything Izmir wanted: he was afraid he would get a second dose of that terrible lance, which Izmir was brandishing in an extremely martial fashion.

The king equipped himself with the queen's arms, and climbed into the bag with Izmir. The finest horse in the stables was brought for Izmir; the king mounted another, and they galloped off as fast as they could to join the army. The queen, at the head of a sizeable squad of ladies, was valiantly defending a bridge across a little river, on the other side of which the enemy was drawn up in battle formation. Crab-apples were flying in all directions; those who suffered the slightest injury withdrew from the fight.

Izmir watched this stirring combat for a moment, then burst out laughing. Sire, he said to the King of Quietlife Island, would you like me to get rid of all those people for you?

Very much, my dear friend, replied the king. No sooner said than done: Izmir gave his horse free rein, passed through the queen's squadron, and – like a torrent rushing down a mountainside – crossed the river and emerged on the other side.

The enemy had not expected such an act of daring. Izmir was so good-looking that they thought at first he was a young woman, but they soon changed their mind when they saw him with his lance in his hand, laying about him, knocking riders to the ground, killing, crushing – in short, wreaking total havoc. The queen had a terrible fright, for Izmir's horse had inspired all the other horses, and they charged across the river with him, despite their riders' best efforts to stop them. The king, seeing that Izmir was taking things seriously and slaughtering his foes without quarter, came running up and took hold of his horse's bridle: What on earth do you think you're doing? he said. Stop, for goodness' sake. You can't kill people like that without mercy. It would be a fine thing if you taught them how to kill as well, and they came and paid us back! All we wanted to do was to chase them away. Look, there's no one left except the ones you've killed or wounded.

Izmir shrugged his shoulders, but he stopped none the less, seeing that they had all run away. He accompanied the king, the queen and the army back to the crystal palace, chatting to them on the way.

Although the prince had just covered himself in glory, he showed no signs of being pleased with himself. He inspected the troops, looking closely at all the ladies in the army in the hope that Starlight might be among them. His search was in vain. He sighed bitterly and fell into a melancholy mood, despite the king's endless talk: with his whispering voice, the king was the most monstrous chatterbox in the land.

Instead of going into the palace again, Izmir made up his mind to pursue his search for Starlight through every country and across every sea in the world. But when he tried to take his leave of the king and queen, the king protested that he could not allow Izmir to abandon them so soon, and he pressed him so hard that he finally agreed to climb back into the absurd bag, and was hauled up again into the palace apartments.

Prince Izmir yielded to this uncalled-for pressure only with the greatest reluctance and disgust, and fell into a black mood. He asked the king why on earth he had no staircase in his house. My predecessors have never had one, he replied. A fine reason for maintaining such a stupid and inconvenient custom! Izmir said curtly.

The king, who had become most submissive to the prince, promised to have a staircase built if he would show him how to do it. Izmir was touched by the king's respectful manner and felt that he should not leave these obedient people in a state of ignorance. He agreed to remain with them for a year, all the more willingly because he thought he was more likely there than elsewhere to hear news of his beloved Starlight. He found some consolation in not being in the place where his love had first blossomed.

He inspected the troops, in the hope that Starlight might be among them.

During his stay on Quietlife Island, an extraordinary change came about in the behaviour of its effeminate inhabitants. He accustomed their ears to noise, gave them some knowledge of architecture, sculpture, and the practical arts. He even attempted to prepare them for warfare: he managed to impose on them some sort of discipline, and taught them how to carry out military exercises and manoeuvres with passable skill. But he was unable to make them resolute, brave or bold. When three different armies suddenly landed on the island, Izmir was delighted to have such a good opportunity for a practical application of his lessons. He mustered his troops and was all ready to lead them into battle; but these cardboard soldiers were unable to stand the sight of the enemy. They were so terrified that they deserted Izmir on the spot. He performed miracles of bravery in order to save the king's life at least. They were both taken prisoner, and the town was sacked. While the enemy were finishing off the job of destroying it and looting its treasures, they had Izmir put in one of their boats, where, having lost a great deal of blood, he fainted.

Izmir remained unconscious for a long time, and when he opened his eyes, he was amazed to find himself alone: the boat was sailing of its own accord. He had, it seemed, recovered all his strength, and his wounds had disappeared. In two days, the marvellous boat brought him to a port which he immediately recognised: it was the harbour that served the capital of his own country.

Some people who were walking past, dressed in clothes of deep mourning, recognised Izmir at once. They helped him out of the boat, and prostrated themselves at his feet, weeping with emotion and crying: God save the king! These shouts of acclamation filled the prince with alarm, and he soon learnt that his parents the king and queen had died of grief, almost simultaneously, because they had lost their son.

Izmir was exhausted and faint with hunger, but he forgot his own troubles and abandoned himself to sorrow. He was moved to the very core of his being: he wept bitterly for his father and mother and asked to be taken at once to their tomb. It was only when his pious sentiments had been satisfied that he put on royal robes and received the homage of the great and the respect of the common people.

Starlight was meanwhile not far from his thoughts. The very next day he sent a distinguished embassy to the yellow forest to inform the centaurs of his accession to the throne, and to ask them to send a thousand of their number for his personal guard.

They were most grateful that the new king should have remembered them in such a friendly manner, and sent the centaurs he asked for. Their leader, who was one of the most prominent citizens of the forest, took him a pigeon and a dove: the pigeon had a talent for finding things that were lost. The moment Izmir heard this, he ordered it to go and look for Starlight; as he felt that one could never do too much to ensure success, he also ordered his senior admiral to put to sea with a fleet of a thousand ships.

The dove never left the king's side; in fact, she generally perched on his shoulder. The centaur-in-chief assured him that she would in due course be the means by which Starlight was recognised.

Several days went by; then Izmir's subjects, seeing him always in a sad and solitary mood, or locked in private conference with the captain of the centaur guards, decided to suggest that they should find him a queen to ensure that the royal line would be continued. The most prominent citizens sought him out and begged him, for his people's sake, to agree to their wishes and give them princes of the blood royal. When Izmir heard this proposal, his heart, where his tender love for Starlight was faithfully preserved, contracted with sorrow, and he wept.

I have no wish, he said, to refuse my peoples the reward they may rightly expect for their devotion to me; but I implore you, dear friends, to give me time to renew my search for Princess Starlight, whom as you know I loved so tenderly. My love for her has done nothing but increase; she fully deserved it, and even if she were not the daughter of the mighty King of Arabia the Blest, her virtues alone would make her worthy of the throne. If in a year's time I am given proof that she no longer exists, you yourselves may choose for me a princess who is to your liking; until then, please do not mention it again, unless you wish to torment me, which I cannot believe.

The representatives of the people humbly prostrated themselves before him and replied that nothing could be more reasonable than what the king had proposed. Fresh ships were equipped and launched with extraordinary speed to search yet again for Starlight in the four corners of the world. When they arrived in a port, or on the meanest shore, the cry went out: *Whoever gives us news of the beautiful Princess Starlight will be rewarded with a fine province, to be presented in person by our king, together with a hundred thousand pieces of gold and a superb horse.*

This magnificent promise attracted wide attention, but there was still no sign of Starlight. The admiral would have become weary of all these fruitless voyages if he had been less fond of Izmir; but he could not make up his mind to return without news of the princess, and so he sailed on.

Meanwhile, the waves had carried Starlight to the shore close to a magnificent city. She was rescued by none other than the king of the country, who happened to be walking along the beach at that moment. The monarch was moved to pity by Starlight's youth and charms, and generously commanded that the beautiful stranger be taken to his palace and that she be looked after as if she were his own daughter. He had once had a daughter, but she had been lost for many years; as he no longer expected to see her again, he made up his mind to adopt the young woman whom fortune had brought to his shores.

So now she was waited on, dressed like a princess, and adored by the whole court. She was treated in the friendliest way by the queen, and even more by the king's son. Starlight was extremely grateful for their expressions of affection, but she could not stop weeping: parties, hunting, tournaments, nothing the king invented to distract her could lessen her grief.

The queen, who genuinely loved this delightful girl, asked her one day why she was so sad. Only the prince royal was with them. Starlight was quite prepared to tell them her misfortunes; all she left out was the secret that Ermine-White had told her to keep. One learns more from experience than from any lessons: she was afraid the fairy would punish her. Starlight painted her love for Izmir in such life-like colours that she touched the hearts of the good queen and the young prince. But when she told them that she was the daughter of the King of Arabia the Blest and that she had been abducted when the town was sacked, the queen threw her arms round her neck, embraced her, and kept saying my darling daughter. The prince was delighted to have found such a charming sister again and went at once to inform the king of this happy discovery. While the queen and the princess were giving free rein to their joy and pouring out their hearts to one another, the good king appeared. Starlight wanted to throw herself at his feet, but he clasped her tenderly in his arms, and there ensued endless embraces, questions, explanations, and other infinitely touching demonstrations: everyone talked at once.

The jubilation quickly spread and was shared by the whole court. Cannon were fired, violins played, there was a banquet with roast pigeons, sweetmeats and preserves, and everyone drank themselves breathless on the most exquisite wines. The rockets, the firecrackers, the marionettes and the common people made a terrific din. Everyone wanted to see the princess at the same time, and they all brought presents – jewels, diamonds, fabrics, little dogs, sheep, monkeys and parrots. Starlight accepted each gift with a kindness and gratitude that was universally applauded, and before taking their leave, everyone was offered a choice of café au lait or redcurrant cordial.

At last the excitement died down, and the princess's thoughts turned once more to her darling Izmir. Her uncertain future cast a shadow over all her pleasures; she sighed, she wept to relieve her feelings, and grieved that she was unable to share this happy event with the prince.

But far worse was to come. Her father granted her hand to his neighbour the Emperor of the Deserts. He had just signed a treaty with this powerful and dangerous monarch, and hoped that the marriage would cement it and bring lasting peace.

The princess thought she would die of grief when she heard this dire news. She threw herself down at her father's knees and maintained that she had promised to be faithful to Prince Izmir and therefore could not possibly belong to another man. The king said she must be deluded. He ignored all her tears and protestations and commanded her to accept the Emperor of the Deserts as her husband. She went time and again to embrace the queen and appeal to her for help; but although the kind woman shared her daughter's grief and tried to console her, she could think of no remedy: Starlight must obey.

The shock and pain of this new misfortune were so great that the princess could neither eat nor sleep. The preparations for her wedding progressed rapidly, and the fatal moment drew near. One night when she was even more distressed than usual, she remembered the little box that Fairy Ermine-White had given her. Her present danger seemed more pressing than the perils she had undergone at sea, and she made up her mind to use the box this time. She opened it.

A dark cloud came out and wrapped itself about Starlight. Quarter of an hour later, the cloud dispersed and she found herself on a ship made of mother-of-pearl; her cabin was lined with silver brocade and hung with mirrors, and the movement of the ship told her that she was on the open sea. Her cabin was lit by a magnificent rock crystal chandelier. Recovering somewhat from her astonishment, she rose from the sofa where she was sitting and found herself looking straight into a large mirror. She was horrified to see that she had turned into an Ethiopian, dressed in Moorish style in silver and rose-pink muslin, with a guitar hanging from a rope of white and rose-pink diamonds round her neck, and belt and buskins to match.

This splendid outfit did not console her for the loss of the loveliest complexion in the world. Cruel, barbarous Ermine-White! she cried wretchedly; even if you have preserved my beloved, how can he still love me beneath this frightful colour? Take my life, if you have condemned me to lose his affection.

She did not stop there: she ran up on deck, determined to cast herself into a watery tomb. As she went, she felt a powerful hand restrain her; she turned, and saw the fairy.

Faint-hearted girl, said Ermine-White, I see that the loss of your beauty has made you seek death, as if beauty were the only thing that could bring you happiness. Alas! replied Starlight in great distress and weeping copiously, I valued it only for the sake of Izmir, and now Izmir won't love me any more. Sobs stifled her voice. But if fate had made your lover's life depend on the loss of your beauty, continued the fairy, what would you have chosen, that he should die, and you regain your appearance, or that he live, but you remain an Ethiopian? That he should live, Starlight replied without hesitation, but that I should die, if he was no longer attracted to me. You shall both live, the charming fairy said, kissing the princess, and you will live in happiness and contentment. So much constancy and such perfect love deserve my protection.

On this, she disappeared, and Starlight stopped worrying about her colour. The little ship sailed gaily on, until at last it entered the port of Izmir's kingdom.

The lovely Ethiopian leapt lightly ashore, and adjusting her guitar, which she played divinely, she passed through the town and made her way to the royal palace.

Izmir was coming down the steps at that very moment to take a walk by the sea, as he did every day, to see if his admiral had arrived, for he had had no news from him.

Starlight recognised the prince at once. Seeing that he wore a crown, and a cloak of black crêpe, she guessed that he was now the king. The only thing that surprised her was that he had a dove on his shoulder. She trembled as she stepped forward to greet him, dropping a curtsey at once alluring and delicate. The young king was charmed by the sparkling and graceful manners of this young Ethiopian woman; the magnificence of her dress convinced him that she must be a personage of importance. This was not all he felt: a secret intuition, known only to true lovers, made him curious, and he approached her eagerly, asking her what had brought her to his court.

Starlight was torn between the ecstasy of seeing her beloved again and the pain of knowing that he did not recognise her: she felt as if she must die. Yet joy, aided by her confidence in the fairy's promises, won the day. Without replying to the king's questions, she tuned her guitar and sang these words (you will see that she composed them on the spot):

> I come from a distant shore
> So that you shall weep no more.
> Your own Starlight, sparkling white,
> For your sake refused outright
> A king, said to be quite smart,
> Who had offered her his heart.
> He was really very hurt,
> But she'll love until she dies
> Izmir's fair curls and dark eyes.
> Your sweet spotless lady friend
> Would much rather bite the dust
> Than betray her lover's trust.
> There my little song must end.

Enchanted by this song, Izmir said to the Ethiopian: Lovely black lady, is it really true that you are acquainted with my dear Starlight, since you assure me that she is still alive?

Hardly had he said these words when the pigeon came flying down and landed on the princess's head. The dove too fluttered its wings, and suddenly Fairy Ermine-White appeared. She touched the Ethiopian with her magic wand and thus spared her the trouble of replying, for she instantly became the faithful, the divine, the enchanting Princess Starlight. Izmir thought he would die of joy and astonishment. He flung himself at the feet of his mistress, who immediately made him rise and prostrate himself at the fairy's feet instead.

Love one another always, my children, as you do now, she said, kissing them both. I have come here especially to bless your true devotion.

Izmir was beside himself; Starlight hardly knew what she was doing: the only feeling she could distinguish amid the whirl of emotion was that she wanted to express her gratitude to the fairy. The king took them both by the hand, and led them to his royal apartment. There, an even greater surprise awaited them: whom should they see but the King, the Queen and the Prince of Arabia the Blest! Ermine-White had brought them there in less than a second by means of that powerful white magic to which all nature must submit. In the most gracious manner imaginable, they consented to let Starlight the Beautiful marry Izmir the Constant, and the wedding was delayed only until the next morning. When Izmir was thus at last united with Starlight, he became as happy a husband as he had been a faithful lover, and they spent the rest of their lives amid endless pleasure and contentment.

"you would fear me less
if you knew me better—"

✳ *The Great Green Worm*

Translated by A. S. Byatt

MARIE-CATHERINE D'AULNOY

There was once a great queen who gave birth to twin daughters, and immediately invited twelve neighbouring fairies to visit, and to make gifts to the little girls, as was the custom in those days – a very good custom, since the power of the fairies set to rights almost everything that nature had spoiled; although sometimes, it must be admitted, this power also spoiled what nature had made perfectly well.

When the fairies were all in the banqueting hall they were served a splendid feast. They were all going to their places when Magotine made her entry; she was the sister of Carabosse, and no less wicked. The queen shivered when she saw her, fearing disaster, for she had not invited her to the feast; but she carefully concealed her anxiety, and herself went in search of a chair, covered in green velvet and embroidered with sapphires. Since Magotine was the senior fairy there, the others all arranged themselves to make way for her, and whispered to each other: We must hurry sisters, to make our gifts to the little princesses, to forestall Magotine –

When she was offered the chair she said rudely that she did not want one, and was quite tall enough to eat standing up – but she was wrong about this, for the table was somewhat high, and she was unable to see over it, since she was extremely short of stature. This quite put her out of temper, and increased her ill-will.

My lady, said the queen, I do beg you to take your place at the table.

If you had wanted me there, replied the fairy, you would have invited me with the others – I see that the only people welcome at your court are beautiful people, fair of face and straight of limb, like my sisters. I myself am far too old and ugly for you – but all the same I have just as many powers as they have – indeed, without boasting, I can safely say I have a few more.

All the fairies begged her so pressingly to join them at the table that in the end she agreed. Then a golden basket was brought in, containing twelve beautiful bouquets of jewelled flowers – the first twelve fairies each took one, and nothing was left for Magotine, who began to mutter unpleasantly, and grind her teeth. The queen flew to her bureau and brought back a Spanish leather case, delicately perfumed, covered with rubies and full of diamonds, and begged the fairy to accept it. But Magotine shook her head and said: Keep your jewels, ma'am – I've got much better ones at home – I only came to find out whether you had remembered me, and I see that you had in fact completely ignored me.

Thereupon she struck the table with her wand, and all the lovely food was changed into snake stew, which upset the other fairies so much that they threw down their napkins and abandoned the feast.

While they were discussing the nasty trick Magotine had just played on them, the savage little fairy went up to the cradle

"Keep your jewels, ma'am,—
I've got much better ones at home"

where the princesses were all swaddled in sheets of cloth-of-gold, most beautiful to behold. I grant you, she said briskly to one of them, perfect ugliness – ; she was going on to pronounce some equivalent malediction on the other, when the rest of the fairies, terribly upset, hurried up to prevent her – to such good effect that the wicked Magotine smashed a large glass window, shot through it like a bolt of lightning, and vanished from sight.

Whatever gifts the well-disposed fairies were able to bestow on the princess, the poor queen was not really able to feel their kindness, since she was wholly possessed by the unhappiness of finding herself mother of the ugliest creature in the world. She took the little thing in her arms and watched miserably as she grew uglier and uglier every moment. She made terrible efforts to control her grief, and to stop herself from bursting into tears in front of the gracious fairies – but the tears could not be kept back, and the fairies were seized with pity for her.

What shall we do, sisters? they asked each other. What can we do to console the unfortunate queen?

They held a great council, and then told the queen to be less overwhelmed by her grief, for a time was to come when her daughter would be greatly happy –

But – interrupted the queen – But will she become beautiful?

We may not tell you any more at present, replied the fairies. You must be content to know that your daughter will be happy.

She thanked them repeatedly, and did not forget to send them away with many presents – for although the fairies were extremely rich, they still liked to be offered gifts, and this custom has since come to be observed by all the peoples of the world, and remains quite unaffected by the passage of time.

The queen called her elder daughter Hidessa, and the younger one Bella. These names suited them perfectly, for Hidessa grew to appear so frightful that, however intelligent she was, it was impossible to look her in the face. Her sister grew prettier and prettier and seemed a most attractive child. The result of this was that when Hidessa was twelve, she threw herself at the feet of her parents and begged them to allow her to go and shut herself away in the Lonely Castle, to hide her ugliness, and to spare them any further misery. They had not given up loving her, despite her deformities, so they felt some reluctance in giving their consent. But Bella remained, which was quite sufficient consolation, so they agreed.

Hidessa asked the queen to send with her only her nurse and a few household servants.

There is no need to be afraid of anyone carrying me off, she told her mother – and I assure you that, shaped as I am, I want to hide away even from daylight.

The king and the queen agreed to her request, and she was escorted to the castle she had chosen. It was centuries old; it was approached from the sea, and its windows opened on foam and breakers; a great forest lay behind it, in which it was possible to ride and to wander, and in another direction lay open meadows. The princess played skilfully on various instruments, and sang wonderfully well. She stayed two years in this pleasant solitude, and even wrote various books of thoughts and meditations. But, in time, she felt a stronger and stronger need to see the king and queen, so she had her horses put to, and travelled to the court. She arrived exactly at the moment when the Princess Bella was to be married. All was joy and festivity. When they saw Hidessa everyone looked upset. Neither of her parents kissed her or hugged her, and the only welcome anyone gave her was to tell her that she had grown considerably uglier, and that she really shouldn't think about coming to the ball – if, however, she wanted just to have a look at it, they might find some little hole or cranny for her to peep through.

She replied that she had not come to dance, nor indeed to listen to the violins – but that she had been so long in the Lonely Castle that she had felt compelled to leave it to pay her respects to their majesties the king and the queen, and that she was now very painfully aware that they could not stand the sight of her – so she would go back to her wilderness, where the trees, the flowers and the fountains made no comments about her ugliness when she came near them. When the king and queen saw that she was so angry, they begged her, at some cost to their own peace of mind, to stay with them for two or three days. But since she had a spirited and generous nature, she replied that she would find it too hard to leave, if she passed so much time in such good company. They were too eager for her to leave to try to hold her back, so they merely replied coldly that they were sure she was perfectly right.

On the occasion of her wedding the Princess Bella gave her sister an old ribbon which she herself had worn all that year attached to her muff, and the king she was marrying gave his new sister-in-law a skirt-length of taffeta, in a harsh purplish-reddish colour called zinzolin.* She felt a fierce urge to throw both the ribbon and the zinzolinnery back in the faces of the very generous persons who offered her such meagre entertainment; but she had so much spirit, so much good sense and so much real wisdom, that she would not let herself show any hint of bitterness. Then she left with her faithful nurse for her Lonely Castle, her heart so full of sadness that she passed the whole journey without saying a word.

*

One day, when she was on one of the darkest paths of the forest, she saw beneath a tree a large green snake, which lifted its head and said: Hidessa, you are not alone in your unhappiness. Look at my terrible face, and know that I was born even more beautiful than you.

The princess, seized by fear, did not hear half these words – she fled, and for several days did not dare to go out, for terror of a similar encounter. In the end, becoming bored with being alone in her room, she came down one evening and wandered along the sea-shore, walking slowly, brooding on her sad fate. Suddenly she saw, coming towards her, a small golden boat, hung about with all sorts of intricate devices. The sail was gold brocade, the mast was cedar, the oars were sandalwood; it seemed to be propelled by chance alone; and as it halted very near the shore, the princess, curious to see all its beauties, stepped inside. She discovered that it was upholstered in crimson cut velvet, on cloth-of-gold, and its studs appeared to be made of diamond. But suddenly the boat sped away from the shore – the princess, in alarm, took to the oars to turn it back, but her efforts were in vain – a wind sprang up, the waves swelled higher and higher, and she was soon out of sight of land. Surrounded by sea and sky, she abandoned herself to fortune – expecting, moreover, that fortune would bring her nothing pleasant, and thinking to herself that Magotine had played this nasty trick on her, as was her habit. I am going to die, she said to herself. What are the secret prickings and shrinkings that make me fear death? What pleasures have I known so far to make me hate it? My ugliness frightens even my nearest relations. My sister is a great queen and I am dispatched to a wilderness where the only company I found was a talking snake. It is better for me to die, than to drag out my miserable days any longer.

These thoughts dried the princess's tears. She looked about courageously to see what side death would come from – she seemed indeed to be asking it not to delay any longer, when she saw riding the waves, a serpent which came near the boat and said: If you felt disposed to accept help from a poor Green Worm, such as me, I am able to save your life.

Death frightens me much less than you do, cried the princess – and if you do wish to please me, make sure I never have to look at you again!

The Green Worm gave a long hiss (that is a serpentine way of sighing) and without reply, plunged beneath the waves. What a loathsome monster, said the princess to herself; he has greenish wings, and his body is all sorts of changing colours – he has ivory claws and his head is covered with a sort of mane of ugly fronds. I really would rather die than owe my life to that creature. And yet, she went on, what makes him want to follow me, and by what mysterious agency does he talk like a rational being?

She was musing in this way when a voice seemed to answer her thoughts, saying: Understand, Hidessa, that you must not despise the Green Worm – and, if it isn't too harsh a thing to say, I would point out that he is much less ugly in his kind than you are in yours – but far from wishing to anger you, we are anxious to comfort your distress, if you will give your consent.

This voice startled the princess considerably, and what it said appeared to her so reasonable, that she was quite unable to hold back her tears. But then she thought to herself – How silly I am not to be able to weep for my approaching death because someone or other points out how ugly I am – even if I were the most beautiful woman in the world, I should perish nevertheless – and *that* ought even to be a sort of comfort to me, and stop me from caring about the life I am about to lose –

Whilst she was moralising in this way, the boat, still floating along at the winds' will, suddenly hit a rock, and shattered into splinters. The poor princess saw that all her philosophy was no use at all against such immediate danger. She reached out for a few planks which she felt herself clasp in her arms, and felt herself borne up, and carried, with great good fortune, to the foot of the huge rock. Imagine her state, when she became aware that she was clinging tightly to the Great Green Worm!

When he saw the state of terror she was in, he went away a little distance, and called to her: You would fear me less if you knew me better – but it is my harsh fate to put terror into everyone I meet – and he threw himself immediately into the water, and Hidessa was left alone on the huge rock.

Whichever way she looked, she saw nothing to alleviate her despair; night was coming on; she had nothing to eat, and nowhere to lay her head. I thought I was about to end my life in the sea, she said sadly to herself, but now I see my last moments will be on this rock – some sea-monster will come to swallow me, or I shall starve to death. She seated herself at the top of the rock. Whilst daylight lasted she looked at the sea, and when the night was upon her, she took off her zinzolin taffeta skirt and wrapped her head and face in it – and so she waited, in great anxiety, for what might come to pass.

In the end she fell asleep, and it seemed to her that she could hear the sound of musical instruments; she decided that she must be dreaming – but after a moment or two she heard singing, and the song seemed to be composed especially for her.

> Let sweet love hurt you –
> His arrows may burn
> But their sharpness and fierceness

Quickly will turn
To softness and sweetness –
Princess, now learn
To let sweet love hurt you
And no longer mourn.

Listening carefully to these words woke her up altogether. What lies in wait for me? she asked herself. Happiness, misery – can there possibly be any kind of good life still to come? She opened her eyes with considerable apprehension, fearing to find herself surrounded by monsters – but what was her surprise when, in place of the wild and dreadful rock, she found herself in a bedroom all panelled with gold; the bed in which she lay was furnished richly enough for the most magnificent palace; she lay and stared, trying to work out where she might be, what might have happened, unable quite to believe that she was truly awake. In the end she got up, and ran to open the glass door which led to a wide balcony, from which she beheld all those earthly beauties made by the combined energies of nature and art – gardens full of wonderful flowers, of glittering fountains, graceful statues, and rare trees; there were forests in the distance, and palaces whose walls were studded with precious stones, whose roofs were pearl, all perfectly wrought. Beyond was a mild and rippling sea, covered with all sorts of craft, whose sails, pennants and streamers ruffled by the wind made a perfectly pleasing picture.

O just Gods! she cried. What do I see? Where am I? What an amazing transformation! What has become of the terrible rock which appeared to threaten the heavens with its frowning crags? Am I still the person who yesterday was about to perish in a boat, and was saved by the aid of a serpent? She spoke aloud in this way; she walked up and down; she stopped; finally she heard some kind of sound in her room; she went in, and saw coming towards her a hundred pagods (small Oriental figures, with nodding heads). They were clothed and constructed in a hundred different ways. The tallest were maybe two feet high, and the tiniest no more than four fingerlengths. Some were handsome, gracious and pleasant; others were hideous, fearsome in their ugliness; they were made of diamond, emerald, ruby, pearl, crystal, amber, coral, porcelain, gold, silver, bronze, iron, wood and earthenware; some without arms, others without feet, with mouths in their ears, squinting eyes and flattened noses – in a word, there was no greater difference between all the creatures who inhabit this world, than there was between these pagods.

Those who made their appearance before the princess were deputies of the kingdom. After having addressed her in a long exhortation, studded with a series of judicious reflections, they told her, in order to cheer her, that for some time they had been travelling through the world, but in order to gain permission to do this from their ruler, they had to make a vow, on leaving, never to speak of their experiences – some of them were even so scrupulous that they were unwilling to move their heads, their feet or their hands – but nevertheless most of them were unable to prevent themselves from doing so. They told her that in this way they ran all over the universe, and that, on their return they delighted their king by telling the tale of all the most secret happenings in the different courts where they were received. This pleasure, my lady, added these deputies, we will also sometimes bestow on you, for we are commanded to forget nothing which might amuse or interest you – instead of bringing you presents, we have come to sing and dance for your delight. And they immediately began to sing the following words, whilst dancing in rounds with basque drums and castanets.

Pleasures bring sweet delight
After harsh pains
Pleasures bring sweet delight
After great fear and fright
Break not your chains
Gentle young lovers
For pleasures bring sweet delight
After harsh pains
Pleasures bring such delight
After great fear and fright.

After your cruel despair
Tomorrow's skies, bright and fair
Bring dawn after night,
Soft-smiling and bright.
Pleasures bring sweet delight
After harsh pains.

When they had come to an end, the deputy who had been their spokesman said to the princess: Here, my lady, are a hundred pagodines who are chosen for the honour of serving you; everything in the world you may desire can be accomplished, provided that you remain amongst us. The pagodines in their turn made their appearance; they were all carrying baskets, appropriate to their heights, full of hundreds of different objects, so pretty, so useful, so well constructed and so richly decorated that Hidessa could not weary of admiring, praising, and exclaiming over the marvels before her. The most prominent of the pagodines, who was a small creature made of diamond, suggested that she should go into the bathing cavern, since the heat of the day was increasing. The princess stepped in the direction pointed out to her, between two rows of bodyguards whose size and expressions were enough to make anyone die of laughing. She found two huge vessels, made of crystal and decorated in gold, full of water whose perfume was so good and so fine that she was astonished; a canopy of cloth-of-gold mixed with green was raised above them. She asked why there were two baths, and was answered that one was for her and the other was for the ruler of the pagods. But, she cried, where is he to be found? My lady, someone said, at present he is at war – you will see him when he returns. The princess then asked if he was married, and was answered that he was not, and that he was so good a prince, and so gentle, that he had so far found no one worthy to be his bride. She did not persist in her curiosity; she undressed and entered the bath. Immediately pagods and pagodines began to sing and to play their instruments – some had theorbos made of walnut-shells, some had viols made of almond-shells – for their instruments had to be proportionate to their stature – but all was so exact, and so harmonious, that nothing could be more agreeable than these sorts of concerts.

When the princess stepped out of her bath, she was presented with a splendid dressing gown; several pagods, playing the flute and the oboe, walked before her; several pagodines came after, singing verses in praise of her; and so she came into a room where her *toilette* was laid out. And immediately pagodine ladies-in-waiting, pagodine chambermaids, began to come and go, dressing her hair, arranging her garments, complimenting her, applauding her – there was no longer any question of ugliness, no zinzolin skirt, no greasy ribbon.

The princess was truly astonished. What, she said, can have brought me such extraordinary happiness? I am about to perish, I am awaiting my death, I have nothing else to hope for, and all at once I find myself in the most pleasant place in the world, the

there was no longer any question
of ugliness.

most splendid place, where everyone seems overjoyed to see me! Since she possessed endless wit and kindness she managed so well that all the little creatures who came near her remained happily charmed by her conduct.

Every day, on rising, she found new clothes, new lace, new jewellery. It was a great pity that she was so ugly, but notwithstanding, she who could not bear the sight of herself, began to find herself less unpleasant, with the help of the great care that was taken in decking her out. There was no time of day when there were not some pagods or other arriving, to tell her about the most secret and the most curious happenings in the world – peace treaties, war alliances, betrayals and partings of lovers, infidelities of mistresses, despairs, makings-up, disappointed heirs, broken marriages, old widows who remarried most unsuitably, treasures uncovered, bankruptcies, fortunes made in a moment; fallen favourites, campaigns for positions, jealous husbands, flirtatious wives, wicked children, cities destroyed – in fine, what did they not come to tell the princess about, for her delectation or interest! Sometimes there were pagods with bellies so blown up and cheeks so puffed out that they were truly startling. When she asked them why they were in this state, they replied: Since we are permitted neither to laugh nor to speak in the world, and since we see there endless ridiculous things, and almost unbearable foolishness, the desire to mock is so strong that we puff up with it – it's a kind of dropsy of laughter, which is cured as soon as we are here. The princess was greatly admiring of the good sense of the pagod race – for indeed, we should all puff up with laughter, if we had to laugh at all the oddities we see.

No evening passed without a performance of one of the best plays of Corneille or Molière. Balls were frequent; the tiniest figures, making good use of their situation, danced on a tightrope in order to display their skills; and then, the meals which were put before the princess might well have been taken for important feasts. They brought her books – serious books, books of courtly love, history books – indeed, days flowed past like moments, whilst nevertheless, to be truthful, all these pagods, with all their wit, seemed to the princess to be almost unbearably small – for often, setting out for a walk, she would put thirty or so of them in her pocket to entertain her; it was the most delightful thing in the world to hear their tiny voices chattering away, higher and clearer than those of marionettes.

A time came when the princess, unable to sleep, said: What will become of me – shall I always be here? My life goes on more pleasantly than I could ever have dared to hope; nevertheless I feel some kind of lack, some need in my heart – I do not know what it is, but I'm beginning to feel that this steady sequence of the same pleasures is losing its flavour. Ah! Princess, said a voice – is that not your own fault? If you were prepared to love, you would quickly understand that it is possible to remain for a long time, with the object of one's love, in a palace, or even in a horrible lonely place, without wishing to leave. Which of the pagodines is speaking to me? she asked. What wicked counsel is she suggesting, endangering all the peace in my life? It is no pagod, replied the voice, who is warning you of something which you will indeed do, sooner or later. It is the unhappy ruler of this country, who adores you, my lady, and who trembles as he finds the courage to say so. A king who adores me! answered the princess. Has this king any eyes, or is he perhaps blind? Has he perceived that I am the ugliest person in the world? I have seen you, my lady, replied the invisible being, and I find you by no means such as you describe yourself to be; and whether because of your person, your virtue, or your misfortunes, I say again, I adore you, but my love, both respectful and fearful, still keeps me in hiding. I am deeply grateful to you, replied the princess, but alas! what would become of me if I were to love anything? You would achieve the happiness of one who cannot live without you, said he, but if you do not give your permission for him to appear, he would not dare to do so. No, said the princess, no, I wish to see nothing which might have too powerful an effect on my emotions. There was no answer to this, and she spent the rest of the night deeply pondering this adventure.

However resolved she was to say nothing at all which might give any indication of this adventure, she was unable to prevent herself from asking the pagods whether their king had returned. They replied that he had not. This answer, which did not fit with what she had heard, made her uneasy. She persisted, and asked if their king was young and handsome; they replied that he was young, handsome, and very agreeable; she asked if they had frequent news of him, and they replied that they heard from him daily. But does he know, she asked, that I am in his palace? Oh yes, my lady, they answered, he knows everything that occurs in your life, he takes a particular interest in it, and we send off hourly messengers who bear news of you to him. She was silent then, and began to dream much more frequently than before.

When she was alone, the voice spoke to her; sometimes she was afraid of it; but sometimes she found it pleasing, for there could be nothing more courteous and amiable than what it said to her. However resolved I am never to love, she would answer, and however strong are the reasons which lead me to defend my heart against an attraction which could only destroy it, I do admit that I should be very happy to make the acquaintance of a king with your bizarre predilections – for if it is true that you love me, you are perhaps the only creature in the world who could feel such a weakness for someone as ugly as myself. Think whatever you will about my character, my adorable princess, replied the voice – I find quite enough reason for my feelings in your virtues. Moreover it is not these things that constrain me to hide myself – I have other causes, and such unhappy ones that if you knew them, you would be unable to withhold your pity. The princess then urged the voice to explain further; but the voice spoke no more, and the princess heard only long, heavy sighs. All these things disturbed her; although this lover was unknown and hidden, he paid her a thousand attentions; and added to this was the consideration that the place where she found herself made her wish for more appropriate company than that of the pagods. And for this reason she began to feel everything around her boring and uninteresting, and to feel that only the invisible voice could occupy her time with pleasure.

On one of the darkest nights of the year, when she had gone to sleep, she was aware, on waking, that someone was sitting beside her bed; she thought it was the pearly pagodine, who, bolder and brighter than the others, sometimes turned up to entertain her. The princess reached out her arms to take her up, but someone grasped her hand, pressed it, kissed it, and let drop a few tears on it, clearly too overcome to speak; she had no doubt but that it was the invisible king. What do you want of me, then, said she to him, sighing – can I love you without knowing you, and without seeing you? Ah, my lady, was the reply – what conditions do you impose on the delight I should feel in giving pleasure to you? It is impossible for me to let myself be seen. The wicked Magotine, who played such a cruel trick on you, has also condemned me to seven years of suffering, of which five have already passed, and two remain – and you would sweeten all the bitterness of those two last years if you would take me for your husband. You are about to decide I am foolhardy, and that what I ask is wholly impossible – but my lady, if you knew the extent both of my passion and of my distress, you could not refuse the gift I ask of you.

Hidessa was finding her life uninteresting, as I have already said, and she found the invisible king very attractive as to his mind and wit, and love took hold of her heart in the deceptive guise of generous pity. She replied that a few days were still needed for her to be able to make a decision. This was already a great step forward, that she should have been brought to the point of putting things off for only a few days, and the feasts and concerts multiplied around her, she heard nothing but wedding songs, and presents were offered to her richer than any she had ever seen. The amorous voice, assiduously accompanying her, courted her through the night, and the princess retired always earlier and earlier in order to have more and more time to entertain the invisible visitor.

At last she agreed to take the invisible king as her husband, and promised not to see him before his years of penitence were at an end. Everything hangs on this, for both of us, he told her; if you were to give way to imprudent curiosity, I should have to begin my years of suffering again, and this time you would have to share them with me; but if you are able to prevent yourself from listening to the bad advice you will be given, you will then have the happiness of seeing me as your heart desires, and at the same time of recovering the wonderful beauty stolen from you by the wicked Magotine. The princess, delighted by this new hope, vowed a thousand times to her husband to feel no curiosity which went against his wishes, and so they were married, without noise or ostentation, whilst hearts and spirits, notwithstanding, found their true satisfaction.

Whilst all the pagods made a great effort to amuse their new queen, there was one who brought her the story of Psyche, recently retold in elegant words by a fashionable author;* she found there many things which seemed to relate to her own adventures, and she developed such a strong desire to have her father and mother with her, and also her sister and her brother-in-law, that nothing the king could say to her would release the grip of this fantasy on her mind. The book you are reading, said he, tells you the misfortunes into which Psyche fell – please, I beg you, learn from that to avoid the same evils. She promised even more than he asked, so that eventually a ship of pagods and of presents was dispatched with letters from the Queen Hidessa to the queen, her mother. She implored her to come to visit her in her kingdom, and the pagods, on this one occasion, had permission to speak when they were not in their own country.

The loss of the princess had not failed to bring out some sensibility in those closest to her; they had believed her to have perished, so her letters were a great happiness to the court; and the queen, who was dying with desire to see her, did not hold back for one moment, but set off with her daughter and her son-in-law. The pagods, who alone knew the way to their kingdom, conducted the whole royal family to the place, and when Hidessa saw her parents she thought she was about to die of joy. She read and reread Psyche, to be put on guard about anything that might be said, and about how she should respond; but she made a hundred mistakes; sometimes she said the king was away with the army, sometimes he was ill, or in such bad-humour that he would see no one, sometimes he was on pilgrimage, and then he was hunting or fishing. In the end it began to look as though she were sworn to say nothing that had any real meaning, and as though the cruel Magotine had completely scattered her wits.

Her mother and sister discussed the situation; it was concluded that she was deceiving them, and perhaps also deceiving herself, so that, with a somewhat ill-directed eagerness they made up their minds to talk to her; they managed to do this so skilfully that they threw her mind into all sorts of fears and doubts; after having spent a long time preventing herself from agreeing to what they said, she did reveal that so far she had never set eyes on her husband, but that his conversation was so charming, that simply to hear him was enough to content her; that he was undergoing some sort of penance for another two years, and after that time, not only would she see him, but she herself would become beautiful as the bright day. Ah, you unhappy creature, cried the queen. What crude snares have been set out for you! Can it be possible that you have such simple faith in such fairy stories? Your husband is a monster, and that is what he has to be, for all these pagods whose king he is are no more than little grubs. I would more readily believe, replied Hidessa, that he is the god of love himself. What folly! cried Queen Bella, they told Psyche she had got a monster for a husband, and she found it was Love himself; you have got it into your stubborn head that Love is *your* husband, and he is quite certainly a monster; do at least set your mind at rest, shed a little light on something so easy to clear up; that is what the queen too argued, and her son-in-law went on in the same way for some considerable time.

The poor princess remained so confused and disturbed that, having seen off her family with presents that very much more than repaid the zinzolin taffeta and the muff ribbon, she resolved, whatever might happen, to see her husband. Ah! Fatal curiosity, which cannot be extinguished in us by hundreds of terrible examples, how much you are about to cost this unhappy princess! She felt it was proper to imitate her forerunner, Psyche, so she concealed a lamp, like her, and then held it up to behold the invisible king, so dear to her heart. But what dreadful screams burst from her when, instead of the young Love, golden, white, young and altogether lovely, she saw the horrid Green Worm, with his long fronded mane standing on end. He woke, consumed with rage and despair. Cruel woman, he cried, is this the reward of so much love? The princess did not hear him, for she had already fainted for fear, and the Green Worm was already far away.

At the sound of all these tragic happenings several pagods had hurried in; they put the princess to bed, and tended her, and when she came round, she found herself in a state imagination can hardly begin to grasp – how greatly did she reproach herself for the harm she had done her husband! She loved him tenderly, but she loathed his form, and she would have given half her life not to have set eyes on it.

However these sad reflections were interrupted by some pagods who came into her room with terrified looks; they came to warn her that several ships, full of marionettes, with Magotine at their head, had entered the port unopposed. The marionettes and the pagods are inveterate enemies; they are rivals in a thousand quarrels, and the marionettes even have the privilege of speaking wherever they are, which the pagods have not. Magotine was their queen; the hostility she felt towards the poor Green Worm and the unfortunate Hidessa had driven her to call together her forces to come and persecute them at the exact moment when their griefs were sharpest.

She had no difficulty in succeeding in her designs: for the queen was so distraught that even when she was urged to give the necessary orders, she would not, saying that she understood nothing about warfare; orders given in her name assembled the pagods in the besieged cities, and the most important captains in the council room – she commanded them to take charge of everything, and retired into her study, looking on, almost with indifference, at the passage of life.

Magotine's general was the famous Polichinelle, who was very competent in his profession, and who had a large reserve battalion made up of wasps, cockchafers and butterflies, who performed wonders against a few lightly armed frogs and lizards. These had been enlisted in the pagods' army a long time ago, and in fact their names inspired more fear than their courage.

Magotine amused herself for some time watching the battle; the pagods and pagodines showed great courage, but the fairy, with a stroke of her wand, dissolved all the splendid surroundings – the lovely gardens, the woods, the meadows, the fountains were buried beneath the crumbled ruins, and Queen Hidessa could not escape the harsh fate of becoming the slave of the most wicked fairy there will ever be; four or five hundred marionettes forced her to come into Magotine's presence. My lady, said Polichinelle, here is the queen of the pagods, whom I bring to you with humility and respect. I am already only too well acquainted with her, said Magotine; she was the cause of an insult offered to me on the day of her birth, which I shall never forget. Alas, my lady, said the queen, I believed you had already taken a great enough revenge for that; the gift of ugliness, which you bestowed on me in the highest degree, might have sufficed anyone less vindictive than you. How she proses on, said the fairy, look at this learned doctor promulgating her new ideas. Your first task shall be to teach philosophy to my ants, so prepare yourself to give them a daily lesson. And how can I set about that, my lady, replied the afflicted queen, – I have never studied philosophy, and if I knew any, would your ants be capable of learning it? Look at her, look at this casuist, cried Magotine. Very well, dear queen, you shan't teach them philosophy, but you *will*, despite yourself, give the whole world some demonstrations of patience which it will be very hard to imitate.

And she promptly sent for some iron shoes, so tight that half the foot could not be squeezed in – and nevertheless they had to be strapped on – the poor queen had more than enough time to weep and to feel the pain. Aha, said Magotine, and now here is a distaff wound with spider-webs – I command you to spin it as fine as your own hairs, and I give you two hours and no more. I have never spun, my lady, said the queen, but, although the task appears impossible, I shall attempt to obey you. So they took her immediately into the depths of a dark cavern, closed it with a huge stone, and left her with a crust and a pitcher of water.

When she tried to spin the filthy spider-webbing, her spindle was far too weighty for the task, and fell to the ground, time after time after time – she had the patience to gather it up, again and again and again, and to begin over and over, but it was all no use. I now see too well, said she, my overflowing misery. I am in the power of the implacable Magotine, and she is not content to have bereft me of my beauty, she is looking for pretexts to bring about my death. She began to weep, revisiting in her imagination the happy state she had enjoyed in the Kingdom of Pagody, and she threw her distaff to the ground. Let Magotine come when she pleases, said she, I cannot achieve the impossible. Then she heard a voice, which said: Ah! Queen, your indiscreet curiosity has cost you the tears you are letting fall: nevertheless it is too hard simply to watch the suffering of those one loves; I have a friend, of whom I have never spoken to you, who is called the Guardian Fairy – I hope she will be able to come to your aid. And immediately she heard three sharp knocks, and although she saw no one at all, she found her distaff full of thread, spun and combed. At the end of the two hours Magotine, intent on picking a quarrel, had the stone set aside from the mouth of the cave and swept in, followed by a whole troop of marionettes.

Let us see, let us see, the work of a lazy creature who knows nothing about needlework and nothing about spinning.

My lady, said the queen, I did indeed know nothing, but necessity taught me.

When Magotine had taken in this curious turn of events, she took the bobbin of spider-thread and said: You are indeed excessively skilful, and it would be a very great pity not to make good use of your talents – and so, dear queen, go and turn this thread into fishing-nets, strong enough to take salmon.

Ah now, for pity's sake, replied the other, it is clear that even flies would be difficult to hold in such nets.

You are a great arguer, my pretty friend, said Magotine, but that will do you no good at all. And she went out of her cave, had the great stone rolled back, and assured the queen that if the nets were not ready in two hours, she was lost for ever.

Oh, Guardian Fairy, said the queen then, if it is true that my distress can move you, please do not deny me your help – and even as she spoke, there were the nets, all ready. Hidessa was infinitely amazed, and in her heart gave thanks to the helpful fairy who did so much good for her, and she thought with happiness that it was doubtless her husband who had enlisted this friend to support her. Alas, Green Worm, she said, you are very generous still to love me after the bad things I have done to you. There was no answer, for Magotine entered, and was truly amazed to find the nets so skilfully worked that no ordinary hand could have crafted them.

And so, said she, are you going to have the effrontery to try to make me believe that it is you yourself who wove these nets?

My lady, said the queen, if I were indeed so bold, you see I am shut away so well that it would be difficult indeed for anyone to speak to me without your permission.

Since you are so clever and so skilful, you will be extremely useful to me in my kingdom.

She immediately ordered her ships to be prepared, and all the marionettes to be ready to sail, and had the poor queen confined in heavy iron chains, lest in some passionate movement of despair she might cast herself into the sea. The unfortunate princess bewept her sad fate throughout a long night, and then, in the light of the stars, she saw the Green Worm, softly approaching the ship. I am still afraid of frightening you, he said, and despite the reasons I may have for treating you with less solicitude, you are still infinitely dear to me. Can you forgive my uncontrolled curiosity? she asked him. And may I say to you:

> O my dear Snake, can this be truly you?
> And do I see again my heart's desire?
> Beloved husband whom I see anew
> After fierce pains, extreme as ice and fire –
> Which torment my poor heart
> When we two are apart.

And the Worm replied with this verse:

> The pains of separation
> Work in our flesh and blood
> Like demons of vexation
> Sent from the hellish nation

Transfiguring what's good
To fright and perturbation
Which torment our poor hearts
When we two are apart.

Magotine was not one of those fairies who occasionally take a nap. The desire to do harm kept her constantly awake, and so she did not fail to hear the conversation between the king-serpent and his wife – she rushed in to interrupt it like a fury. Aha! said she, now you are whining in verse, and complaining away like the Lord of the Muses – that warms my heart – Proserpine, who is my greatest friend, has asked me to present her with a poet for her to employ – not that she hasn't got plenty, but she seems to want more. And so, Green Worm, I command you, as the final task of your penance, to go to the dim dwelling, and make my compliments to the gentle Proserpine. The unfortunate Serpent departed immediately with long hisses, leaving the queen in the deepest grief; she thought there was no more to be done; and cried out desperately: What crime have we committed to bring down your wrath, barbarous Magotine? I was hardly in the world when your infernal curse took away my beauty and made me loathsome. Can you claim that I was guilty of anything? since I was not yet a reasonable being, and had no idea of my own identity. I am sure that the unhappy king you have just dispatched to the Underworld is as innocent as I was – so end it now, give me my death at this instant – that is the only grace I ask of you.

You would indeed be too happy, said Magotine, if I were to grant your request – but first you must draw water from the bottomless well.

As soon as the ships had arrived at the kingdom of the

marionettes, the cruel Magotine took a millstone, hung it around the neck of the queen, and bade her climb, so encumbered, to the top of a mountain whose summit was high above the clouds; when she was there she was to gather four-leaved clover, and fill her basket with it, and thereafter she was to descend to the depth of the valley, in order to draw, in a pitcher full of holes, the Water of Discretion, and to bring back enough of that water to fill the great glass of Magotine. The queen said that it was impossible for her to fulfil this command; that the millstone was ten times her own weight; that the leaking pitcher could never hold the water the fairy desired to drink, and that she could not bring herself to undertake so impossible a task. And if you fail, said Magotine, rest assured that it will be your Green Worm who will suffer for it. This threat so terrified the queen that she did try to walk; but alas! it would have been quite hopeless, if the Guardian Fairy, whom she called on, had not come to her aid. The fairy said, as she arrived: Now you see the just reward for your fatal curiosity – do not complain, except to yourself, about the state to which Magotine has reduced you; and immediately she carried her to the mountain-top and filled her basket with four-leaved clover, despite the dreadful monsters who guarded it, who made quite supernatural efforts to defend it; but with a stroke of her wand the Guardian Fairy rendered them milder than lambs.

She did not even wait for the queen to thank her before completing all the good she was able to do for her. She gave her a little chariot, drawn by two white canaries, who both talked and sang beautifully; she told her to go down the mountain, and throw her iron shoes at two giants armed with clubs who were guarding the fountain, and they would fall to the ground, senseless; that she should give her pitcher to the little birds who would be able to find a way to fill it with the Water of Discretion; and that as soon as she had it, she should wash her face with it, and she would immediately become the most beautiful person in the world. The fairy advised her not to stay near the fountain, nor to go back on to the mountain, but to stay her steps in a pretty little wood which she would find along her path; and there she could spend three years; for Magotine would believe that she was still trying to catch the water in her pitcher, or that the other perils of the journey had destroyed her.

The queen embraced the knees of the Guardian Fairy, and thanked her a thousand times for the great kindnesses she had received from her; but, she went on, neither the happy outcome you promise, nor the beauty I may receive, could give me any joy until the Serpent is unserpented. And that is what will happen, after your three years in the wood near the mountain, said the fairy, when you have finally given the water in the leaking pitcher and the clover to Magotine.

The queen promised the Guardian Fairy to fail in nothing she had set out for her to do. And yet, my lady, she added, shall I be three years without a word of the serpent-king? You deserve to spend the rest of your life without word of him, replied the fairy; for can there be anything more terrible than to condemn this poor king, as you have done, to begin his penance once more? The queen made no answer, but the tears which streamed from her eyes and her silence were sufficient evidence of the pain she was in. She got into the little chariot, the canary birds did their work, and brought her to the depth of the valley, where the giants guarded the Fountain of Discretion. She quickly took her iron shoes and threw them at their heads; as soon as they were hit, they fell lifeless as statues; the canaries took the leaky pitcher, and mended it with such extraordinary skill that it appeared never to have been broken. The name which the water bore aroused in her a desire to drink it; it will make me, said she, more prudent, more discreet, than in the past. Alas! If I had had these qualities I should still be in the Kingdom of Pagody! And after drinking a long draught, she washed her face, and became beautiful, so beautiful, that she appeared more like a goddess than a mortal.

And immediately the Guardian Fairy appeared and said: You have just done something which makes me infinitely happy; you knew that this water could give beauty both to your soul and your body, and I wanted to see which of the two was more important to you – in the event, it was the soul that won, for which you have my admiration – and this good deed will shorten your penance by four years. Please do not take away any of my pain, said the queen, for I deserve it all, but give comfort to the Green Worm, who deserves none. I will do what I can, said the fairy, and embraced her – but now you are so beautiful, I desire you to abandon the name Hidessa, which is quite inappropriate, and I wish you to take the name of Discretion. And with these words she vanished, leaving behind a tiny pair of slippers, so pretty and so delicately embroidered that the queen was almost sorry to put them on.

When she got back into her chariot, holding her pitcher full of water, the canaries took her directly to the mountain wood. There never was a more pleasant place; myrtles and orange-trees joined their branches to make long covered alleys, and little woody chambers where the sun never penetrated; a thousand streams and springs which flowed softly helped to freshen this lovely dwelling, but the most remarkable thing was that all the animals could speak, and that they gave the warmest welcome in the world to the tiny canaries. We thought, said they to them, that you had abandoned us. The time of our penance is not yet exhausted, replied the canaries, but here is a queen whom the Guardian Fairy has sent here in our charge – please help to entertain her as well as you can. And at that moment she found herself surrounded by animals of all kinds, who received her with great courtesy. You shall be our queen, said they, and we shall care for you and honour you in every way. Where am I? she cried, and by what supernatural power are you able to speak to me?

One of the little canaries, who never left her side, whispered in her ear: You should know, my lady, that several fairies, having set out to travel, were distressed to see human beings who had fallen into truly bad ways – they thought at first that it would be enough to give warnings, to tell them to mend their ways; but their concern was of no avail, and they suddenly grew irritated, and imposed penances on the wrongdoers; those who talked too much became parrots, magpies and hens; lovers and mistresses became pigeons, canaries and lapdogs; those who imitated their friends became monkeys; certain people who were too fond of good food became pigs; the angry turned into lions – indeed the number of people they transformed was so great that this whole wood is inhabited by them, and you will find people of all kinds and of all dispositions.

From what you have just told me, my dear little canary, said the queen, I have reason to believe that you are here only because you loved too well. That is true, my lady, replied the canary. I am the son of a Spanish grandee. Love in our country exercises such power in our hearts that when it takes hold of us, we fall into the crime of rebellion. An English ambassador arrived at the court, with a wonderfully beautiful daughter, whose arrogance and sharpness were nevertheless quite unbearable; however, I became attached to her, indeed I loved and worshipped her; sometimes she seemed to respond to my attentions, and sometimes repulsed me so fiercely that she exhausted my patience. One day when she had cast me into despair, a dignified old woman came up, and reproached me with my weakness; but everything she said only made me more stubborn, which she saw, and she became angry. I condemn you, said she, to become a canary bird for three years, and your mistress shall be a wasp. And at once I felt a strange change coming over me, the most extraordinary you can imagine; despite my affliction I was unable to prevent myself from flying into the ambassador's garden, to see what had become of his daughter; I had hardly arrived when I saw her coming towards me in the form of a wasp, buzzing four times louder than all the others; I tumbled around her with all the ardour of a lover whom nothing can deter; she made several attempts to sting me. If you desire my death, lovely wasp, said I, there is no need to use your sting – you have only to command me to die and I shall do so. The wasp made no answer, but set about the flowers, who had to endure her bad temper.

Overcome by her scorn and my own state, I flew on without setting any particular course. I arrived eventually in one of the glorious cities of the world – the one they call Paris – I was weary, I threw myself down amongst the leafy branches of some tall trees in a walled enclosure, and without knowing who had trapped me, I found myself inside a cage, painted green and decorated in gold; the furniture and the dwelling were of a startling magnificence; and immediately a young person came to caress me, and spoke to me with so much sweetness that I was enchanted; I did not stay long in her chamber without learning the secret of her heart; I observed that she was visited by a swaggering bully, always in a rage, who was impossible to soothe, and not only overwhelmed her with Injust accusations but beat her so cruelly as to leave her almost dead in the arms of her waiting-women; I was immoderately afflicted myself to see her suffer such unworthy treatment; and what distressed me still further was that it appeared that all the blows he showered on her had the effect of arousing all the tenderness of this lovely young woman.

I wished day and night that the fairies who had transformed me into a canary would arrive and impart some sort of order to these ill-assorted *amours*; my desires were fulfilled; the fairies appeared suddenly in the chamber just as the enraged lover was beginning his usual exercises; they heaped him with reproaches and condemned him to become a wolf; as for the patient woman who allowed herself to be beaten, they turned her into a sheep and sent them both off to the mountain wood; for my own part, I was able to find an easy way of flying off. I had a wish to see the different courts of Europe. I travelled through Italy, and chance put me into the hands of a man, who, since he was frequently absent on business in the city, and wanted to prevent his wife, of whom he was very jealous, from seeing anyone, locked her up carefully from dawn to dusk, and intended for me the honour of amusing this beautiful prisoner – but she was occupied with quite different concerns than my entertainment. A certain neighbour, who had long been in love with her, came every evening by the rooftop and slid down the chimney, arriving blacker than a demon. The keys employed by the jealous husband had no use beyond assuring his own peace of mind; and I was in perpetual fear of some embarrassing catastrophe – and then the fairies made their way in through the keyhole, causing no small astonishment to these two amorous persons. Away with you to do penance! they said, touching them with their wands, so that the chimney-sweeper became a squirrel, and the lady a little monkey, for she was clever, whilst the husband who was so keen on guarding his house, became a bulldog for ten years.

I would have far too long a tale to tell, my lady, added the canary, if I described all my adventures; but I am required from time to time to come back to the mountain wood, and I rarely come without seeing new animals, for the fairies continue to travel, and people continue to affront them with endless failings; but for the time you are here, you may be much diverted by the tales of all the adventures of the people who find themselves here. Several offered on the spot to tell her all about themselves as soon as she desired; she thanked them very civilly; but she was more in need of reflection than of conversation, and sought out a lonely place where she could be by herself. The moment she had decided on it, a little palace appeared, and she was offered the most delightful feast in the world; there was nothing but fruit, but rare and wonderful fruit, brought to her by the birds – and all the time she was in the wood, she wanted for nothing.

There were sometimes celebrations more remarkable for their oddity than for anything else – lions could be seen dancing with lambs, bears murmured sweet nothings to doves, and snakes addressed themselves gently to linnets. There was even a flirtation between a butterfly and a panther. That is to say nothing was arranged according to species, for it was not a question of tiger or sheep, but simply of persons the fairies desired to punish for their faults.

They loved Queen Discretion devotedly; all made her the judge in their disputes; she was absolute ruler in the little republic, and if she had not reproached herself incessantly with the misfortunes of the Green Worm, she might have been able to bear her own with a kind of patience; but when she thought about the state she had brought him to, she was unable to forgive herself for her indiscreet curiosity. When the time came to leave the mountain wood, she alerted her little guides, the faithful canaries, who assured her she would have a happy return; she stole away in the night, to avoid the farewells and the regrets which would have cost her some tears; for she was touched by the friendship and the respect which all these thinking beasts had offered her.

She forgot neither the pitcher full of the Water of Discretion nor the basket of clover nor the iron shoes; and, just when Magotine had concluded that she was dead, she appeared before her, the millstone round her neck, the iron shoes on her feet, and the pitcher in her hand. The fairy, on seeing her, uttered a great shriek; and then demanded where on earth she had come from? My lady, said she, I have spent three years fishing for water in a leaking jug, and at the end of that time I found a way of making it stay there. Magotine burst out laughing, thinking of all the weariness the poor queen must have undergone, and then she looked at her more closely. What do I see? cried she. Hidessa is grown altogether charming! and where did you obtain all this beauty? The queen told her that she had washed herself with the Water of Discretion and that this marvel had then come about. On hearing this Magotine in a fit of despair threw the pitcher on the ground. O Power that defies me, she cried, I shall be avenged! Prepare your iron shoes, said she to the queen, for you must go on my behalf to the Underworld and ask Proserpine for the tincture of longevity; I am always in fear of falling sick and even of dying; but when I have that antidote I shall have no further cause for concern – only make sure that you leave the seal on the bottle untouched, and do not taste the syrup she will give you, for you would lessen my dose.

The poor queen had never been more surprised than she was by this command. What is the way to the Underworld? she asked. And is it possible for those who go there to return? Alas, my lady, will you ever weary of persecuting me? Under what star was I born? My sister is much happier than I am; it is impossible to believe that the constellations dispense all fates equally. She began to weep, and Magotine, full of triumph at the sight of her falling tears, burst out laughing: Come, come, said she, do not for one moment delay a journey which will bring me so great a satisfaction; and she filled a scrip for her with mouldy walnuts and crusts; and with these delightful provisions she set off, resolving to smash her head against the next rock to put an end to her troubles.

She travelled on for some time in no particular direction, starting out one way, making a turn in another, and thinking that it was quite unheard-of, to be commanded to set out for the Underworld. When she got weary, she lay down at the foot of a tree and began to dream of the poor Worm, taking no further thought for her journey, when suddenly she saw before her the Guardian Fairy, who said: Are you aware, lovely queen, that in order to bring back your husband from the dark place where he is held at Magotine's behest, you will have to go to the dwelling of Proserpine? I would go even further, if it were possible, replied the queen – but my lady, I do not know how to make my way down to those shadowy regions. Look, said the Guardian Fairy, here is a green branch – strike the earth with it, and recite these verses clearly. The queen clasped the knees of this generous friend, and then said:

*

O you who can disarm the Thunderer's might
  Dear Love, come to my aid!
  Behold how I am made
A plaything for the Fairy's cruel spite.
Lead me, I pray, into the land of Night,
For in that darkness still your flame burns bright.

Your power has worked in Pluto's dreadful breast
Proserpine's hand smooths that dark brow to rest,
Lead me, sweet Love, into the land of Night.
My dear love has been cruelly stol'n away
My sad eyes cannot bear the light of day,
  In pain I cannot draw each breath
  Yet cannot come to Death.

She had hardly finished her invocation when the most beautiful boy in the world appeared in the midst of a cloud of mingled gold and azure; he flew down and came to rest at her feet; his head was crowned with a garland of flowers; the queen knew from his bow and arrows that he was Love himself, and he said to her:

> I have heard your cries
> And come through the blue skies
> To dry the tears that glisten in your eyes.
> I shall stand your friend
> The Green Worm's pain shall end
> To the Dark World together we'll descend
> To bring your husband back into the light
> And to confound the Fairy's cruel spite.

The queen, dazzled by the brilliance which surrounded Love, and delighted by his promises, cried:

> I am prepared to follow you to Hell
> To see the husband whom I love so well.
> And I shall find that dark and loathsome place
> Pleasant and bright, if I can see his face.

Love, who rarely speaks in prose, struck three blows, singing these words with perfect expressiveness:

> O Earth, open your jaws
> Love bids you, let us go
> To that dark realm below
> Governed by Pluto's laws.

Earth obeyed, opened her wide womb, and through a dim path, where the queen was in great need of a guide as brightly shining as the one who had taken her into his care, she arrived in the Underworld; she was afraid of meeting her husband there in his serpentine form; but Love, who upon occasion takes trouble to perform kindnesses to the unfortunate, having foreseen all that would be required, had already ordered matters so that the Green Worm should return to the form he bore before his penance. And whatever Magotine's powers, alas for her, what could she do against the power of Love? So that the first thing the queen came upon was her gentle husband; she had never seen him in this lovely form, and he had never seen her looking so beautiful as she had now become – nevertheless, a kind of presentiment, and perhaps Love, which was the third of their company, made it possible for them to guess who they both were. The queen immediately said to him, with great tenderness:

> I come to bend the iron bars of Fate
> Quick to release you from your prison'd state
> And join two hearts that none shall separate.
> So Hell, which others shake with fear to see
> Holds neither pain nor terror now for me.

The king, carried away by intense passion, replied to his wife with all possible delight and joy; but Love, who dislikes wasting time, urged them to appear before Proserpine. The queen offered the fairy's compliments to the goddess of the Underworld, and asked her to grant her the gift of the tincture of longevity. Now this was a kind of password between these goodly persons; so the goddess instantly gave the queen a small flask, not very well stoppered, to encourage her to try to open it; but Love, who was not new to this game, warned the queen to hold back from a curiosity which could still be fatal; and hurrying away from these dismal surroundings the king and queen came back into the light of day. Love had no desire to abandon them, so he himself took them into Magotine's presence, and, to keep himself unseen, hid in their hearts. Nevertheless, his presence stirred up such unaccustomed good nature in the fairy that, although she had no idea why, she was very graciously disposed to these noble sufferers, and making a supernatural effort of generosity, she gave them back their Kingdom of Pagody. They returned there without more ado, and lived the rest of their lives as prosperously as they had so far endured misery and disgrace.

> Insidious curiosity
> Gives rise to evils of a hateful kind.
> On secrets which can shatter heart and mind
>   Why cast an eye?

> This madness burns most hot in womankind –
> Call the first Woman (and the Snake), to mind,
> Model for Psyche and Pandora who,
> Eager for knowledge that the gods had hid,
> Uncovered hissing evils and so did
> Harm to themselves and harm to others, too.

> Hidessa shed intrusive light
> On the invisible Worm, by night,
> Which hurt them both, and this despite
> The warning clear in Psyche's story
> Which was still fresh in her memory.

The moral is, that humans cannot learn
To be discreet, from stories or the past,
But stubbornly experiment, and burn
Their fingers in old flames, and come at last
To give advice to others in their turn
Which others, in their turn, forget as fast
As did Hidessa, those Greek Gods, and Eve.
Ponder well, Reader! Now I take my leave.

 GLOSSARY

The White Cat

* Rodillardus: Bacon-gnawer, the name of a cat borrowed by La Fontaine from Rabelais, see 'The Rats' Council', Fables II, 11.

* Minagrobis: An echo of La Fontaine's Raminagrobis in 'The Rat League', Uncollected Fables, which were only published posthumously, in 1696, i.e. not long before Mme d'Aulnoy wrote her tale. Grobis: Old French word for a haughty cat.

* Martafax: Another echo of La Fontaine, 'The Battle of the Rats and the Weasels', in which the doughty warrior rats are called Artarpax, Psicarpax and Meridarpax. Fables IV, 6.

* Lhermite: Another nod in the master fabulist's direction, cf. 'The Rat who Retired from the World', Fables VII, 3.

* tilting at the ring: In this chivalrous variation on the tourney, the contestants do not drive at each other with lances lowered, but at a hoop or ring (often beribboned).

* Sinbad: John Ashbery's only 'liberty' with the text, which has

'Perroquet' for the parrot's name. As *The Arabian Nights* were soon to appear in Antoine Galland's influential translation (1704–17), Sinbad seemed an apt anticipation.

The Subtle Princess

* Count Ory: the hero of a medieval legend from Picardy, who inspired Eugène Scribe and Charles Gaspard Delestre-Poirson to write a one-act vaudeville play (1817), which Rossini then used for his opera buffa, *Le Comte Ory (1828)*.

* Regulus: Roman consul executed by Carthaginians c.250 BC: his eyelids were cut off and he was left to stare at the sun, then rolled in a spiked barrel.

Bearskin

* *Letters of a Peruvian Lady*: *Lettres d'une Péruvienne* by Mme Françoise de Graffigny (1695–1758) which appeared in 1747. Unless this passing tribute is an interpolation, it also suggests that the story was attributed to Mme de Murat afterwards.

The Counterfeit Marquise

* M. Pellisson: Paul Pellisson (1624–93), lawyer and writer, friend of Mlle. de Scudéry, mocked by Molière, and famous for his high principles.

* D'Aleteff – Possibly a scrambled version of Mme de Lafayette's name, and hence a possible tongue-in-cheek reference to the author of *The Princesse de Clèves*.

* Prince Sionad: Adonis, anagrammatically – paragon of masculine charms.

* afterpiece – A theatrical convention of the period: see R. W. Bevis, ed., *Eighteenth-century Afterpieces* (Oxford, 1970).

* *violons* – The King's private string orchestra: consort of twenty-four violins.

Starlight

* Lapiths and Centaurs: At the wedding feast of Pirithous and Hippodamia, the drunken Centaurs attempted to abduct the bride and her Lapith attendants and friends, whereupon a terrible battle broke out; in many interpretations, the conflict symbolised the struggle between the human (Lapiths) and the animal (Centaurs).

The Great Green Worm

* zinzolin: a reddish-violet colour associated with cheap, woven fabrics; the poet Paul Scarron (1610–60), husband of Mme de Maintenon, introduced it into French in his burlesque poem *Virgile travesti*. It sounds as if it could be related to the English linsey-woolsey, meaning a coarse cloth.

* the author referred to is La Fontaine, who in 1669, published a story, *The Loves of Psyche and Cupid*. Corneille, Molière and Quinault were also to take up this episode from Apuleius's *Golden Ass* to make a tragedy-ballet from it in 1671.

NOTES ON THE AUTHORS, THE STORIES
AND THE CONTRIBUTORS

Marie-Catherine Le Jumel de Barneville, Baronne d'Aulnoy
(c. 1650–1705)
   Born Normandy, into family with literary connections;
   married François de la Motte, Baron d'Aulnoy; the marriage
   was unhappy and the couple separated. Had four children,
   including one or two later. Published three volumes of travels
   and memoirs of Spain and England, supposedly based on
   experiences, though this is doubtful. First novel, *Histoire
   d'Hippolyte, Comte de Duglas* published to acclaim in 1690;
   her salon flourished thereafter. Produced several volumes of
   fairy tales 1690–1705, which were immediately translated into
   English and other languages. Famed for her wit, beauty, high
   spirits. Faded from view when children's literature experts
   decreed her frivolous.

'The Great Green Worm': 'Le Serpentin vert', first appeared
within the frame novel, *Dom Fernand de Tolède*, in *Contes
nouveaux* (Paris, 1698).

'The White Cat': 'La Chatte blanche', in *Contes nouveaux, ou, Les Fées à la mode*, Vol. 2 (Paris, 1698).

Marie-Jeanne L'Héritier de Villandon (1664–1734)

From a Parisian family with Norman connections; her father was one of the king's many official historiographers, her mother a cousin of Charles Perrault. Poet, historian, *salonnière*; published several miscellanies which included her pioneering fairy tales. Wrote panegyrics to her close friends Madeleine de Scudéry, and Antoinette Deshoulières, feminists and women of letters like herself; inherited Scudéry's salon after her death. Did not marry, possibly out of principle.

'The Subtle Princess': 'L'Adroite Princesse, ou, Les Aventures de Finette', first published in *Oeuvres meslées* (Paris, 1695).

Henriette-Julie de Castelnau, Comtesse de Murat (1670–1716)

Born Brittany; her father governor of Brest; aged sixteen, married to the Comte de Murat; made close friends with L'Héritier and other *salonnières* and writers of fairy tales in Paris. Strong temperament, fantastic taste in dress, outspoken; published many collections during her exile from the capital for a thinly disguised satirical fable about the king's love affair. Also prosecuted by her husband's family for unruliness; reprieved after Louis XIV's death, but back at last in Paris, died of kidney stones.

'Starlight': 'Etoilette', and 'Bearskin': 'Peau d'Ours', appeared in the novel, *Les Lutins du château de Kernosy* (Paris, 1753, 2nd edition); republished in *Voyages imaginaires, songes, visions, et romans cabalistiques*, Vol. 35 (Amsterdam and Paris, 1789). As the stories are added to the novel after Murat's death,

Lubert (*c.* 1710–*c.* 1779). Cf. Mlle de Lubert, 'La Princesse Lionnette et le Prince Coquerico', 'Le Prince Glacé et la Princesse Étincelante', and 'La Princesse Camion', *Le Cabinet des fées*, Vol. 33 (Paris, 1785); see also Zipes, *Beauties, Beasts*, op. cit., pp. 226–56. Future volumes of *Wonder Tales* hope to include Lubert.

Charles Perrault (1628–1703)

Published, 1697, aged 69, most famous, founding collection of fairy tales, *Contes du temps passé*. Otherwise his literary efforts unread today; they include autobiography, poems, polemic, panegyrics to the king and other great men of France. *Académicien*, but progressive: supported the cause of women and of the Moderns in the Quarrel of the Ancients and Moderns. Close to his cousin, L'Héritier, with whom he developed the modern fairy tale.

François-Timoléon, Abbé de Choisy (1644–1724)

Born Paris, lived as the 'Comtesse de Barres' and enjoyed numerous clandestine liaisons (with women); sent as envoy to Siam, found religion, and became a priest. His frank *Mémoires pour servir à l'histoire de Louis XIV*, published posthumously, include many surprises.

'L'Histoire de la Marquise–Marquis de Banneville': 'The Counterfeit Marquise', appeared anonymously in *Le Mercure Galant*, Février, 1695. For the controversy about authorship, see Jeanne Roche-Mazon (1928), and Paul Delarue, 'Les Contes merveilleux de Perrault. Faits et rapprochements nouveaux', *Arts et Traditions Populaires*, Nov. 3, 1954, pp. 251–74, esp. pp. 253–62. I am very grateful to Jacques Barchilon for his help; he disagrees however with the attribution, so any error remains my own.

Translators

Gilbert Adair has written three novels, *The Holy Innocents*, *Love and Death on Long Island* and *The Death of the Author*, two sequels to classics of children's literature, *Alice Through the Needle's Eye* and *Peter Pan and the Only Children*, and several volumes of criticism. His translation of Georges Perec's 'e'-less novel, *La Disparition*, has recently been published.

John Ashbery is one of the most prolific and challenging of American poets. His most recent books are *And the Stars are Shining* and *Can You Hear, Bird*. He is currently Professor of Literature at Bard College. Among many other awards, he won the Pulitzer Prize in 1976 for *Self-Portrait in a Convex Mirror* and the 1992 Ruth Lilly Poetry Prize.

Ranjit Bolt worked as an investment adviser for eight years before taking up translation full time. His translations include *The Learned Ladies* and *Tartuffe* by Molière, *The Marriage of Figaro* and *The Barber of Seville* by Beaumarchais, *The Illusion* and *The Liar* by Corneille and *The Double Inconstancy* by Marivaux.

A. S. Byatt is an award-winning novelist and critic. Her novel *Possession* won the Booker Prize and the *Irish Times*/Aer Lingus International Fiction Prize in 1990. Her other fiction includes *The Shadow of the Sun*, *The Game*, *The Virgin in the Garden*, *Still Life*, *Angels and Insects* and *Babel Tower*. She was appointed a CBE in 1990.

Terence Cave is Professor of French Literature at the University of Oxford and Fellow of St John's College. He is also a Fellow of the British Academy. His publications include *The Cornucopian Text: Problems of Writing in the French Renaissance* (1979), *Recognitions: A Study in Poetics* (1988) and a translation of Mme de Lafayette's *The Princesse de Clèves* (1992).

Illustrator

Sophie Herxheimer, a young London-born artist, trained in painting at Chelsea; her work has been widely exhibited and collected. She uses a variety of media – painted paper collages, oil paint, Indian ink – and has designed and illustrated several book jackets, notably the autobiography of Nobel Peace Prize-winner Rigoberta Menchu Tum.

✳ BACKGROUND READING

Aulnoy, Mme d'. *La Cour et la ville de Madrid vers la fin du XVIIe siècle*, including *Relation du voyage d'Espagne and Mémoires de la cour d'Espagne*, ed. B. Carey (Paris 1874–6).

Barchilon, Jacques. *Le Conte merveilleux français* (Paris–Geneva, 1975).

Benjamin, Walter. 'The Storyteller', in *Illuminations*. Trans. H. Zohn (London, 1970), p. 122.

Carter, Angela. Ed. *The Virago Book of Fairy Tales* (London, 1991) and *The Second Virago Book of Fairy Tales* (London, 1992).

Cromer, Sylvie. '"Le Sauvage": Histoire sublime et allégorique de Madame de Murat', *Merveilles et Contes*, Vol. 1, No. 1, May 1987, pp. 2–19.

DeJean, Joan. 'Salons, Preciosity, and Women's Influence', in Denis Hollier, ed., *A New History of French Literature* (Harvard, 1981), pp. 297–303.

Delarue, Paul. 'Les Contes merveilleux de Perrault. Faits et rapprochements nouveaux', *Arts et traditions populaires*, Nov., 3, 1954, pp. 251–74, esp., pp. 253–62.

Dictionnaire de Biographie française, eds. J. Balteau, M. Barroux, M. Prévost (Paris, 1941).

Foulché-Delbosc, R. Intro., Marie-Catherine d'Aulnoy, *Travels into Spain* (London, 1930).

Lougee, Carolyn. *Le Paradis des femmes: Women, Salons and Social Stratification in 17th-century France* (Princeton, 1976).

Palmer, Nancy and Melvin. 'English Editions of French *contes de fées* attributed to Mme d'Aulnoy', *Studies in Bibliography*, 27 (1974), pp. 227–32.

Ravaisson-Molion, F. *Archives de la Bastille* (Paris, 1866), Vol. VII, pp. 335–7.

Robert, Raymonde. *Le Conte de fées littéraire en France de la fin du XVIIe à la fin du XVIIIe* (Nancy, 1982).

Roche-Mazon, Jeanne. 'Une collaboration inattendue au XVIIe siècle: L'Abbé de Choisy et Charles Perrault'. Mercure Galant, Vol. 15, No. 1, 1928: 513–64. *En Marge de 'L'Oiseau bleu'* (Paris, 1930).

Saint-Évremond, Charles de. *Oeuvres Mêlées*. Ed. Charles Giraud (Paris, 1866), Tôme III, pp. 415–16.

Scott, R. F. H. *The Memoirs of the Abbé de Choisy* (London, 1974).

Schiebinger, Londa. *The Mind Has No Sex? Women in the Origins of Modern Science* (Harvard, 1989), p. 156.

Storer, Marie-Elisabeth. *La Mode des contes de fées* (Geneva, 1928).

Thelander, Dorothy R. 'Mother Goose and Her Goslings: The France of Louis XIV seen through the Fairy Tale', *Journal of Modern History*, 54, Sept. 1982, pp. 467–96.

Warner, Marina. *From the Beast to the Blonde: On Fairy Tales and their Tellers* (London and New York, 1994).

Zipes, Jack. Trans. and intro., *Beauties, Beasts & Enchantments: Classic French Fairy Tales* (New York, 1989); *Spells of Enchantment: The Wondrous Fairy Tales of Western Culture* (New York, 1991).